SEMI-DETACHED SATANISTS

BY

GERARD WHITE

The LICHFIELD PRESS

SEMI-DETACHED SATANISTS

BY

GERARD WHITE

First published by
The LICHFIELD PRESS
2001

Copyright Gerard White 2001

Gerard White has asserted his right under the
Copyright, Designs and Patents Act 1988
to be identified as the author of this work.

This novel is a work of fiction. Names and characters
are the product of the author's imagination
and any resemblance to actual persons,
living or dead is entirely coincidental.

All rights reserved.

Jacket design by the author

ISBN 0 905985 29 X

The LICHFIELD PRESS
City House, 2 Dam Street,
Lichfield, Staffs., WS13 6AA

The characters of
SEMI-DETACHED SATANISTS

The Coven

George Whitehouse (myself), 39, married, no children, schoolmaster, High-Priest.

Agnes Upton ('Aggie'), 51, married, one daughter, High-Priestess, a true believer.

Jenny Smirke, 29, Aggie's daughter, husband left her, one son, another true believer.

Helen Meade, 27, married, two children, a tease and a trouble-maker.

Jim Meade, 28, her husband, craft teacher, a good-natured ox.

Maurice Clundon, 46, one son, lay preacher and JP, a snide.

Ron Harvey, 41, senior wages clerk, married, no children, a case of suppressed violence.

Annette Hamlyn, 36, divorcee, two children, ex-model, a self possessed sophisticate.

Molly Batters, 39, married, two sons, a pink pampered pudding,but nice.

The Others

Hilary Whitehouse, 35, my wife, an attractive, bright, brittle, bored woman.

Wayne Smirke, 7, Jenny's son, a snotty-nosed little brat.

Fleur Clundon, 41, Maurice's wife, a compendium of affectations.

Sandra Harvey, 40, Ron's wife, a house-proud, frigid hen-pecker.

Alfie Batters, 40, Molly's husband, automobile expert, a Flash Harry.

'Peter Quince', an elderly maiden lady, herbalist and potential poisoner.

Tom Tydeman, elderly herbalist's assistant and handyman.

Simon Chubb, youngish, a writer in occult periodicals.

Mick Melly, Kate Steinweg, Cy Clark, Ted Pullman, Frank Fielding, Oliver Molloy, Pam Doone, Tim Burke, Petrena Howth, Mike Howth, Peter Copley, Dick Orange, Debbie Smith, Tina Jacobs, Jack Turner, the Faery People.

Jane Acres, 40, married, four children, a fat gossip.

Ann Grimstock, 46, married, one daughter, a very fat gossip.

Dorothy Hines, 43, married, one graceful daughter, a malicious gossip.

Ida Harkness, 44, married, one elephantine daughter, another malicious gossip.

Teresa Rolls, 32, married, two children, cubmistress, a straitlaced Catholic.

Norris Whittaker, 55, Head of George's school, a pompous fraud.

Ethel James, 60, school secretary, a dragon.

Sgt. Freddie Osborne, 38, village bobby, a man susceptible to housewives.

Rev. Hugh Somerhayes, M.A., 50, vicar of St Stephen's, a beanpole.

Rev. Peter Sandiland, age indeterminate, Baptist minister, a smoothie.

Father Michael O'Halloran, 35, priest at Our Lady of Perpetual Succour, a shockheaded Irish lad.

Edmund Wheate, 42, psycho-analyst, a man of magnetic personality.

Chapter 1

AN OWL hooted. Quite close. Good, it pleased me. So appropriate on this evening of all evenings. I tried to make it out but the trees at the roadside grew close and thick and most of their branches were lost in shadows. Shadows Also most appropriate. I snapped open the catch of my briefcase and checked that the all-important document was there. I'd a few miles to go back if I'd forgotten to put it in. No, there it was safe and sound, wrapped around my *athame*. My own *Book of Shadows*. No slavish reproduction, but a work of art. I know that traditionally a witch is supposed to make his or her own hand-written copy of the Book, but I was of course, in no position to do this when I first became a witch. And what a work it is.

I wound down the window of the car and stared into the darkness. No hope of seeing the owl. Perhaps it would cry again? The night scent of vegetation was strong in my nostrils, the air cool and a trifle damp, the moon obscured by banks of low cloud. Earlier, the plumes of vapour rising from the Rugeley power station cooling-towers were faintly wafted from the south-west, promising a mild night. Conditions were good. The one thing I'd feared, rain, now seemed unlikely.

The moon, though I could not see her, would now be full. I could feel her swollen presence. Tonight is the night, I told myself, the night of the esbat. My fourteenth esbat. And next month, August, Lughnasadh! Third of the four main festivals, and one which I intend shall be memorable, to put it mildly!

As for this present meeting, well, we shall see. A new member to initiate. Splendid! And the ritual is elastic, merely a tool for my own amendments easily made on the spur of the moment. And why not, since the ritual, which is steadily growing, becoming enriched monthly (weekly, even) is my own creation. As is the coven itself – my own creation. As are the people – my creations, my puppets, my ... But, steady now, my lad, you're beginning to sound like Frankenstein. We mustn't let our tongue run away with us, must we? We don't want to end up babbling, drooling like a maniac, do we? Of course not. We might put people off, and that would be terrible. They've barely recovered from that business with the gamekeeper, or whoever he was.

Now, a few moments to collect our thoughts, to clarify our mind concerning tonight's business.

I was still thinking when I switched on the ignition, shifted into first gear and bumped back on to the lane. Narrower and narrower and winding like a corkscrew, not a good place to meet another vehicle head-on. Not that there'd be anything much using this road. Most people who wanted to get to Stafford wouldn't go by this route. But then they wouldn't be likely to have business in the wood to the south of the village, as I did.

The wood itself was not over-large and, I guessed, was privately owned. Though I doubted its owner ever visited it. Once it must have been part of the mighty sprawling Cannock Chase, but was now separated from it by some miles of low-lying fields.

I turned off on to an overgrown cart-track and edged my way in under trees until I came to a level spot on dry leafy earth. I took out my briefcase, diving my hand inside once again to feel the silkiness of my robe, the crackly parchment of the Book, the keen cutting edge of my athame, and the various shapes of the rest of my precious paraphernalia.

Emerging from the shelter of the trees I started up the slight rise. At the top, a natural depression in the ground was ringed by trees. It was not visible until one stood upon the very tip of it. A modest fire, I calculated, would not been seen from lower down.

Cradled in the hollow was a stone circle. Not an authentic circle, to my disappointment, but one cobbled together from odds and ends, including a large lump of concrete and a chunk of mortared bricks. These were mossy, and bore no sign of recent usage.

I wished that *my* circle, as I already thought of it, could have been like the Rollright Stones, that splendid circle in Warwickshire, a circle of grotesque, brooding figures, jagged and fantastically scored by centuries of wind and rain. I wished it could have had a grisly history.

The Rollrights had witnessed a brutal ritual murder, so the story goes. A farm labourer was supposed to have been hacked to death with a billhook and finally impaled upon the same implement, in revenge for having spied upon secret rites being enacted within the stone circle.

A colourful tale. I lost no time telling it to my disciples, as if it were an account of what had happened here, at this vastly inferior site. I relied upon their ignorance, to swallow it. Surprisingly, they did.

In the half-light, the hollow, *my* hollow, took on a decidedly spooky aspect.

I even had to repress a slight shiver myself as I stepped into the ring.

Alone. Good. Time to prepare. I selected a place where I would mark out a ring with my athame. A new ring within an old one: a new rite to be enacted upon ground already hallowed by ancient ones. Very fitting, very pleasing. Never before since I started the coven had I had so strong a feeling of the rightness of everything. Tonight would be a good one, a splendid dress-rehearsal for the big one, for the sabbat, for Lughnasadh.

The sound of a car engine disturbs my thought. It slows, revs as its driver slips the clutch to negotiate rough ground, and dies suddenly. I wait, curious to see who will come. Who'll be the first to keep our appointment?

A figure emerges from between two of the tallest stones. A woman, well-made and wearing a pink dress with a white stole about her shoulders. Good Go! Surprise, surprise. The plump and sweet-smelling Molly Batters! She's breathing heavily from the climb and her eyes are like saucers as she looks fearfully around the circle.

"You've come! My dear, I'm delighted to see you!" I exclaim in my best Vincent Price tones, as I seize both of her hands and enfold them in mine.

"Oh yes. But it's been such a ….. Oh, dear! (pant, pant). Such a rush. And so difficult! What with washing the boys' hair, and Alfie asking me awkward questions every time I go out, even if it's only to my friend Judy's! And really, I'm not at all sure that I ought to have come".

"Nonsense, Molly. Don't worry, it'll be quite all right. You'll find it most _interesting_. And I assure you you'll come to no harm." I feel like Svengali saying this, and I'm glad I didn't have time to don my ceremonial rig, otherwise the poor creature might have been scared out of her wits when she first saw me.

"I won't be expected to, to do anything, you know, horrible. Will I?"

"Well, I don't quite know what you mean, my dear. Perhaps you're still thinking somebody might do something horrible to _you._ But let me

"I'm scared. And I don't mind admitting it!"

"Not the slightest need. I promise you. Besides, there'll be one or two people you know coming along."

"Oh? Who?"

"Patience, Molly . Ah, there's another car. Listen. Two cars, if I'm not mistaken. You'll soon see who they are."

Fifteen minutes and we are all assembled.

Before I do a kind of roll-call for your benefit, I should mention that we all have special witch-names (all except Molly, who will be given hers during her Initiation). Names proved to be rather troublesome, until I hit on the idea of Latin names for the men, based upon whatever it was they considered to be their own particular personal qualities. Aggie, our High-priestess, decided upon flower names for the women. Some of them favoured the Latin, some the English.

This night there are nine of us all told.

No question of being genteel and putting myself last: I'm the High-priest, so naturally I come first.

My name is George Whitehouse. I'm 39, married, no children, schoolmaster by profession; witch-name, Felix. Three men are also present. Maurice Clundon, 46, married, one son, executive, lay preacher and magistrate, a snide, in my opinion; witch-name Justus, for obvious reasons. Ronald Harvey, 41, senior wages clerk in a big firm, married, childless, a case of suppressed violence, worries me stiff; witch name, Fortis. And Jim Meade, 34, married, (wife also present, though I don't really approve, as husbands-plus-wives tend to make for inhibition. In fact, I'm thinking of running two covens, to separate husbands and wives, if the need arises, dependent of course upon recruitment.) Jim has one son, one daughter, Art teacher, an old sheep but a thoroughly nice chap; witch-name, Peritus.

Now for the women. My High-priestess is Agnes Upton, 53 married, one daughter (also present), witch-name, Buttercup, would you believe! Next, Annette Hamlyn, 36, divorcee, ex-model, one son, one daughter, a tarty piece; witch-name, Primula. Helen Meade, Jim's missus, 32, part-time teacher, somewhat neurotic; witch-name, Erica   Jenny Smirke, 29, *was* married, but her husband, a former stage magician, did a vanishing trick two years ago. She has one son, is rather a weirdie; witch-name, Poppy. And, finally, sweet plump Molly Batters, 39 married, two sons, housewife, pampered and a wee bit petulant we must admit, our proposed Initiate; witch-name to be chosen from various possibilities up Aggie's sleeve.

The business of the evening: one an Initiation; two, a ritual Invoking of aid for each member's special purposes.

The five women take themselves off behind the stones to make ready. We men go to the opposite side of the ancient circle, remove our clothes, place them in neatly-folded piles. I put on my robe, and we stand waiting for the women to rejoin us.

After my third esbat I had ruled that this should be so, as the sight of women undressing tends to, ahem, disturb the equilibrium of the gentlemen. And I'm damned if I'll allow distraction from the correct observance of our Rites! In fact, to deal with premature excitation

Buttercup keeps a willow wand handy, and should any male organ rear its head inappropriately she has my strict orders to flick it into submission! Can't have the mere acolytes enjoying lewd sensations. That is the High-priest's privilege alone.

We stand in a widely-spaced ring. Molly is told to hang back behind the stones until the High priestess fetches her.

Gathering up the folds of my robe in my left hand, I drive the sharp point of my *athame* into the ground with my right and begin to mark out the first circle.

Jim had driven a stake into the ground where I had indicated and now with the aid of a cord attached to it and looped around my ritual knife I scuttle along backwards carving the turf. I make three circles, the first having a diameter of nine feet, the second and third each a foot wider in diameter. As there is to be Invocation too I quickly inscribe the triangle of Solomon, , its sides tangential to the outermost circle. Whilst Poppy and Primula lay out ropes along the cuts – not an easy job, in the gloom – I offer a prayer of purification.

The witches, my witches, enter the circle. I myself stand at the centre, my robe swathed closely about me to make me look taller. Maurice, Ronald and Jim are stationed at three of the cardinal points, Jenny Smirke (Poppy) at the fourth. Annette and Helen take up positions alternate to the men. We all stand rock-still, as Buttercup goes to find Molly.

She peeps out timidly from between the stones, and contrary to the terms of our preliminary instruction is still wearing a garment, a pink frothy slip. Buttercup tells her to remove it. She does so, reluctantly, and allows herself to be led towards us.

At the edge of the circle the pair of them halt. I bend my gaze impressively, magisterially I might say, upon Molly and command that the ritual bathing be done. Buttercup has a sponge in a plastic bag with which she symbolically wipes Molly's forehead, breast, thighs and feet, before blindfolding her with a strip of black material.

I realise that I've never seen Molly's body at full length before, though I've enjoyed her five times, thrice on the back seat of my car, once under an oak tree and once on her dining-room carpet while Alfie was out. She's definitely the earth-mother type: wide child-bearing hips, big thighs and fine full breasts not normally guessed at owing to the unflattering cut of her dresses and the unsuitability of her bras. I feel a twitch and a stir beneath my robe. And I'm not the only one. Ron Harvey has a tense look about him and is turning away to hide what is certain to be an incipient erection. I give Buttercup an imperceptible nod and she at once focuses her beady eye upon him. Good. I'm not standing for that dirty-minded devil mucking up the Rite. Suddenly his hunched shoulders sag and he turns his head to stare away into the dewy darkness.

But one of these days... he could break out again.

At my command, Buttercup, High-priestess, looking oddly schoolgirlish and haglike at the same time on account of her mini-robe and her wrinkles, ushers Molly into the charmed circle. I ask her in plain words – in conversational style, that is, instead of in the inflated rhetoric of my priestly utterances – if she wishes to change her mind. She quivers, deliciously to my mind, as she replies that she 'doesn't think so.'

"We must be a little more definite," I insist. "This is, after all, only a mild and first form of lowest-degree Initiation. I did explain to you, didn't I, Molly? You will not be a witch in the full sense. You will not be given the seven working tools of the Craft. But you will be able to be present at our Rites and to gain all the benefits which the rest of us gain from them. Well, most of them, at any rate. Do you still wish to join us, or don't you?"

"I , er, yes," she answers, at last.

"Good. Then stand perfectly still. You will hear us dancing and chanting around you. Just hear and be still. Relax. Relax completely." I feel a bit like a stage hypnotist as I say this, but the feeling passes when the whole group begins to dance, widdershins of course, around the inner part of the circle chanting the 'Eko, Eko, Azarak.'

11

Hackneyed, the long-standing student of the occult may say. I can almost hear the sneers. Well, they can go to hell. I think it's an extremely useful chant, and I notice they don't offer any substitutes in any of the mags such as *Batwing,* or *The Practical Occultist.*

Over Molly's plump satin-white shoulder I watch as my witches whirl past. Annette moves beautifully as befits a former actress and dancer, Jenny and Helen are both graceful and hip-swaying. The men spoil the effect somewhat: Jim lumbers around awkwardly like a bear, Maurice Clundon minces a little on his tippy-toes, though I don't believe he's a fairy, Harvey strides along flexing his muscular thighs as though he's progressing down the bathside towards the high diving boards. But, Christ, their voices! Helen sounds sweet, and especially pleasing is Annette's voice. But Jenny might as well be in the fish market. Clundon aims for an effect mid-way between his renderings in the Baptist Chapel and a gypsy serenade, Jim croaks like an old bullfrog, and Harvey sounds like an NCO giving a squad of recruits a bollocking. I add my own well-modulated tenor in an attempt to inject a little dignity. Unfortunately this inspires Buttercup to join in with a noise like a tormented parrot! I hope there's no wanderer in this neck of the woods to hear us. We gasp out a final chorus:

Eko, Eko, Azarak.
Eko, Eko, Zamilak,
Eko, Eko, Cernunnos,
Eko, Eko, A cradia!

The votive altar is a jagged lump of stone, embedded in the earth, lying like a great tooth on its side.

The dancers are still. Back in their starting-places, they face inwards, all of them except Annette Hamlyn panting heavily. I plant myself in front of the altar in ritualistic pose, my parted legs firm like the pillars of life, my trunk erect for the tree of vitality, my arms outflung for justice and mercy. In a deep and dramatic voice I address the postulant.

"Hear me. Hear my secret Name. I am Felix."

"I hear," whispers Molly, prompted by Buttercup.

"And hearken, Oh you Ancient Ones," I continue, lifting my face to the sky, "O Gods of Earth and Air, Fire and Water, O Lords of Night, now heed our Rite. See, the Rune of Proclamation is here made." I hold aloft my Book of Shadows. opened at the page where runic letters declare our intention to initiate.

I turn to Molly, now bound with cords at arm and ankle, her soft, pampered flesh is deep-scored where it is bound around at her waist and above and below her breasts. A phrase from *My Secret Life* floats into my mind: 'enough to raise the cock on a corpse.' But no time for drooling now. Work to be done!

Holding my Book at arm's length, I recite:

"Thou who art standing upon the threshold of the world of Spirits, thou who knockest at the gates of the Ancient Ones, thou who approaches unto the most dread and sovereign Lords, hast thou made firm resolve?"

"I – " begins Molly, until Buttercup outs her off by placing a finger on her lips. Then she, the High-priestess, picks up her sword from the altar and directs it to a point above the postulant's heart. At this, my own heart jumps, for Buttercup's arm is unsteady, her judgement of distance poor without her glasses which she insists upon discarding, and the sword point is needle-sharp. If either she, or Molly, swaying now she's unsupported, should slip! I hurry on:

"For verily I say, rather shouldst thou fall upon this magic blade (talk about asking for trouble!) and die, than enact a falsehood, tell a lie, or fear our holy and our good intentions."

I await her answer. "I have two, " hisses Buttercup, like a prompter to a stage-frightened actress.

"I have two - " says Molly mindlessly. (My God, how true! I mutter to myself. Two of the most luscious, delectable...But steady, lad! I stop myself, recalling the holy nature of my office.) "I have two words, er, perfect words. Perfect love and perfect trust."

"Then you are welcome, thrice and nine times welcome," I intone.

Buttercup lays her sword upon the altar, and leads Molly forward two paces. She embraces her hastily and whispers into ear.

"Now is the time for the naming of your Name," I declare.

"Rosa," murmurs Molly.

"Then Rosa you shall be. The Rose of this coven." I make it sound solemn, though I can't help being annoyed with myself for uttering such a conventional flowery compliment. Not in the spirit of the ritual at all. I must stick to the written formula, I remind myself.

Still blindfolded, Rosa, as she now is, is led to the North, South, East and West of the circle. Then the dancers whirl round again, chanting, to raise the Cone of Power. They have grown chilly with waiting and now step out vigorously to warm themselves. The moon breaks through briefly between banks of cloud and smiles down upon our Rite. Jenny Smirke contorts her body wildly, as if she's got the power, and Buttercup, her mother, is jigging about on the spot behind Molly's back. I can't feel anything myself – but then, *I* don't expect to.

I rapidly consult my Book. At the end of the dance, it says, where I've written the rubrics in red ink, in a florid hand, there follows the 'sexual and purifying ordeal.' Ah, good! The best part! This is the part of the Ritual which I continue to subject to thoughtful amendment and improvement. And to which I shall continue to devote my best efforts in the way of research and the fruits of my inventive mind.

But this time I'll have to tone it down considerably. Curse it! Though it's the only way: I can see our initiate dithering, doubtless from fright more than from cold. But some day, I hope and pray, we shall get hold of one of these game-for-anything chicks, and then... ah yes, then I shall really indulge myself a little. For the present, however, mildness is the thing, mildness and reassurance.

Buttercup crossed to the altar and seizes a large metal phallus, fashioned secretly by Jim in the Metalwork shop at his school. She holds it aloft, it being the symbol of our next act.

With a whispered warning to Molly I begin the Ritual Kiss-blessing. First I kneel before her and kiss her feet, such pink and dimpled toes,

14

but icy against my lips. Then her chubby knees, also dimpled. Next, her genital area. I am reminded of previous initiations as I incline my head to do this, of how Aggie/Buttercup 'blessed' Ron Harvey, taking a full thirty seconds over it while he almost burst a blood vessel, of how I myself 'blessed' Jenny and how she grasped my hair nearly tearing a clump of it from out of my scalp. No lingering this time, though. No exploring tongue. Only a chaste and holy pressure vaguely in the right direction. The breasts I lightly brush each nipple. The lips I feel her heavy, slightly asthmatic breathing in my face, and feel the tremors running through her body.

And now I draw her down to kneel facing me, her knees touching mine.

"Token intercourse with the High-priest," I murmur.

"Oh! Oh! I couldn't! Not in front of other people!" she protests.

"*Token*, Molly, merely *token!*" I remind her, drawing my cloak around us both. I urge her to kneel tall, and press our loins briefly together. "Ritual Scourging," I whisper and help her to her feet. "Don't worry," I add, "there'll be no pain."

Buttercup hands me the scourge and holds the initiate steady while I circle round behind her. I raise the lash and bring it down lightly upon her buttock.

Now, although you'll not believe me, I can honestly say, hand on my heart, that this does absolutely nothing for *me* whatsoever. But I notice a flicker of interest in Clundon, and as for Ron Harvey, he's positively twitching! Definitely kinky, that man. Bottled-up violence, frustration and kinkiness, a lethal combination. I only wish I could think of some way to drop him.

Half a dozen light strokes and I hand the scourge back to our High-priestess. I order the removal of the blindfold from Molly's eyes. She looks bewildered as she gazes around at us.

"The Oath of Secrecy and Loyalty," I announce. "Repeat after me: I do now most solemnly swear,"

"I do now most solemnly swear," echoes Molly.

"by the Lords of Earth and Air, Fire and Water,"

"by the Lords of Earth and Air, Fire and Water,"
"and before these here present,"
"and before these here present,"
"never to reveal any matter pertaining to this coven,"
"never to reveal any matter pertaining to this coven,"
"and never to effect aught but good towards its members or even to wish the same."
"and never to effect aught but good towards its members or even to wish the same."
"I.O. Evo He. Blessed Be."
"I.O. Evo He. Blessed Be."
Molly is now embraced in welcome by all members of the coven. Helen fetches a basket of cakes which she has baked specially for us, and Jim uncorks a demijohn of his own excellent homemade wine. We have a choice of Elderflower or a drier wine made from grape concentrate. We drink from turned hardwood bowls, also Jim's handiwork, and pour out libations to the Old Gods, a touch inspired by the High-priest's studies in Classics. Sounds impressive, but actually refers to O-level Latin and Greek which I took when I was thinking of doing an arts degree.

Several bowlsful later I decide to postpone the Invocation until a later meeting. We all sit crosslegged around the altar to drink, men and women placed alternately. I'm rather tickled to see Harvey trying to fumble Helen Meade who cold-shoulders him, whilst at the same time Buttercup, the only woman present whom he doesn't fancy at all, is stroking his hearthrug of a chest and getting more and more amorous with every drop she drinks.

I spend a few moments caressing Molly and when I next look up it's to find Harvey clasping Buttercup as if he's riding pillion. This puts me in mind of something I read recently: 'the dancing over, the witches give themselves over to copulation with the Devil in the form of a goat who couples with all the women, the beautiful ones from the front and the ugly ones from the rear.'

Considering Molly's newness I think it wiser not to allow things to degenerate into a general orgy on this occasion, so I organise them into a circle and get them moving, to the left as usual. Slightly drunk, I begin the final chant. Buttercup, with her better memory for the words and her unmistakeable fervour, takes over as leader:

> *Queen of moon, Queen of Sun,*
> *Queen of heavens, Queen of stars,*
> *Queen of waters, Queen of earth,*
> *Bring to us the Child of Promise.*
>
> *Great Mother, who gives birth to him,*
> *Lord of Life, born again,*
> *Darkness and tears set aside,*
> *The sun shall come up early.*
>
> *Golden sun of the mountains,*
> *Illumine land, light up the world,*
> *Illumine seas, illumine rivers.*
> *Be sorrow laid, be Joy unfurled.*
>
> *Blessed be the Great Goddess,*
> *Without beginning, without end,*
> *Extending to eternity,*
> *I.O. Evo. Blessed Be.*

The Rite ended, I announce the date of our next meeting. We gather up all our equipment, and dress. I take Molly's arm as we walk downhill in a group to the cars. No broomsticks, flying ointment, etc., for us – but a Volvo, a 4 x 4 , two Peugeots, a Rover and a Mini to whisk us away to our respective homes. As doors slam and engines roar I arrange to meet Molly tomorrow at our usual trysting-place.

My driving's not very good and I nearly go off the road at a sharp bend. Sobering, I reflect on the night's business. Not bad, but there's Better things in store. I shall produce inspired plans for Lughnasadh!

17

Come a long way, haven't we? I tell myself aloud. A long way since the dull old days when …. Yes, it'd be about four months ago when I first woke up to the possibilities of the Craft.

Chapter 2

I WAS sick. Looking back on those days, I've no doubt about it. No, I'm not referring to my witchy activities, but to the time before that. Of course, many people would regard witchcraft as sick, especially as practised by people like me. Or perhaps even more so when practised by its most earnest devotees?

Anyhow, the fact is that until four months ago I was sick. And for how long before that? Years, rather than months. Yes, nearly four years.

Hilary and I have been married six years. The first two were splendid. Probably the only time when I've been really happy. And I'm sure she was happy too, then.

We lived in North London, in a cheap furnished flat in a seedy district and discovered that we'd got a fair amount of money to play with. We were both teaching, and I already had a senior post. So, we not only saved the deposit on a house in double-quick time but were also able to lash out on clothes, good food and entertainment. We went up the West End two or three times a week. Films were our chief enthusiasm: matinee oldies, late night Indian, Japanese or Swedish. Fellini, Antonioni, Bergman were our heroes. We read a lot, stretched out on the carpet with a bottle of wine to hand or a Cona full of black coffee. We played elaborate word games and marathon sessions of Bezique. I remember my mania for scoring. I kept all our results in a red notebook, with highlights such as top score for a hand, for a card, game aggregates, best scores of the week, etc., distinguished with different coloured ball-pens. There wasn't a tremendous amount of sex, but we were definitely *together*. We had the usual stock of private jokes and the kind of private language that intelligent lovers have. We missed each other during the working day.

It was not until we'd moved into our new house, a rural semi at the end of the Piccadilly Line, that the rot began to set in.

Hilary began to grow frigid. Just like a man, you may say, to lay the blame on his partner. But that bit was true. She *was* frigid. For my part, I became mildly perverted: I bought 'feelthy postcards', I hung about at the bottom of neighbours' gardens in the dusk watching lighted windows through my telescope, I played with myself in the Public Library, wrote lurid stuff on lavatory walls. Pathetic! But then, as I said, I was sick.

This situation would never have arisen if only we'd had children. I wanted Hilary to come with me to the doctor and discuss it, but she wouldn't. There might have been some simple solution. Perhaps she felt ashamed because it was her fault? Or, more likely, angry because she thought *I* thought it was her fault? Well, it must have been her, because I was all right. My sperm always came hot and thick and copious as a jug of white sauce. Couldn't have failed to make a baby! Whereas she often didn't come at all.

The biggest breach, though, was caused by my *unfaithfulness*. Yes, I was unfaithful to Hilary. Not with another woman, but with something far more devastating – with Music!

At the age of thirty-six I suddenly discovered Music

Unfortunately, at the same time as I was discovering it I saw it to *inflict it* upon Hilary. No sooner had I learned the superiority of the Beethoven odd-number symphonies than Hilary had a lecture on them. When I began to explore the anguished world of Mahler, Hilary had to endure the vast length and loudness of his works. As I pounded the keyboard – I bought a piano for £3 – on my way up through Hours with the Masters towards the easier Bach preludes and classical sonatas, so Hilary's eardrums suffered. By the time I had climbed to the rarified atmosphere of the string quartet her nerves must have been in shreds. But worst of all, I should think, was her 'widowhood.' You hear of fishing-widows and golfing-widows, yet at least they only suffer, if at all, from the absence of their husbands. Hilary suffered doubly, because although I completely abandoned her on the mental level, my physical presence was still with her, and making an abominable row into the bargain.

There's also the point that had I been unfaithful with another woman Hilary could have done something about it. She could have found ways to win me back, have made herself more attractive, subtly hinted at the other woman's faults, or even have scratched her eyes out! But Bach, Mozart and company were something quite beyond her. Their perfection only underlined Hilary's imperfections. One might as well attempt to fight against the gods.

This situation continued after our move to the Midlands. Originally the move was made because Hilary wanted to be closer to her ailing parents who lived in Lichfield. But, unhappily, they both died shortly afterwards.

I found a teaching job in a large village to the north-west of Lichfield. Also we found a house in the same village. The advice to teachers is, usually, don't live near to where you work. I was to discover the wisdom of this, as time went on.

Although the village seemed rather cut off, it was not too long a journey by car to such shopping meccas as Rugeley, Stafford, Uttoxeter, Burton-upon-Trent, as well as to Lichfield itself.

She must have suffered, I now realise, before she gave me up in the end as a bad job. It's not surprising that she took to going out a lot. Not surprising that she literally fell into the arms of the first man who showed interest in her.

This was Freddie, Sergeant Freddie Osborne, to be precise - baker's delivery man and long-serving member of the district Specials. Long serving wooer-in-extraordinary-of-bored-and-frustrated-housewives, I should add. It must have been clear to him that Hilary came into that category, because when she changed to having Townley's bread,

Freddie's firm, after a quarrel with another baker's man, he started paying her attention from the word go.

"You want to watch him, mate!" advised Ron Harvey. We were out on the drive under the bonnet of my car with Harvey lecturing me on carburation, when Freddie's van drew up.

"What're you talking about?" I asked.

"Him, Osborne," he said, jerking a thumb. "That bloody van's round here as soon as your missus gets back from work. Every lunch-time. People are talking, y'know."

"Oh, they are, are they? Who in particular? Who's been talking to you?"

"I don't need nobody talking to me, mate. I've seen for myself. I've had the week off, as you know, and I've seen the bugger round here every day."

"Thanks, I'm sure," I said dryly. Actually, I knew. Only a few days before I'd tackled Hilary about it.

"Where are you going?" I'd asked.

"Out," she replied, putting on lipstick.

"What, at this time of night? It's quarter past ten."

"I feel like a breath of air."

"But you hardly need to tart yourself up like that. Nobody's going to see you in the dark."

"You never know," she remarked, wearing a Mona Lisa smile. Then she went out and I heard the click of the Yale as she pulled the front door to, and the clop-clop of her heels fading down the road.

I put the fourth movement of Mahler No. 9 on the hi-fi, settled myself in my chair, and got my pipe going nicely.

It was nearly midnight when she came back. I could feel the look of disgust on her face without looking up, as she entered the room and noticed the empty beer cans beside my chair and the ashtray full of matchsticks and dottle.

"Oh, my God! What an awful fug in here!" she said.

22

"You've been reading Norman Mailer again, my dear."

"And what's that supposed to mean?"

"He's an American novelist, darling *The Naked and the Dead,* amongst other novels. 'Fug' is the G.I.s word for our good old Anglo-Saxon F-U-C-K."

"Very literary, I'm sure."

"Where have you been?"

"For a walk. I told you."

"You're not very wet," I observed, eyeing the few spots on her shoulders, "and it's been bucketting down for the past hour."

"Marvellous! The armchair Maigret!" she sneered.

"You're not wet because you've been in Freddie Osborne's car. That's it, isn't it?"

She gave me a long searching look, drew off her gloves and shook out her raincoat. I made a mild protest as a number of drops spattered on to my CD case, disfiguring Georg Solti's face.

"If you must know, yes," she said, after a long pause. "Yes, I have. Do you mind?"

Well, I'd be damned if I was going to give any sign that I minded. Though I must admit that this absolute confirmation of what I'd already suspected jolted me considerably. I said 'no', I didn't mind. She gasped at this reply, glared at me, and then pursing her lips went into the kitchen to make herself a cup of coffee.

Two emotions conflicted in my mind as I opened a last can of beer. Part of me was upset at the idea of Hilary, *my* wife, going with another man, letting him do things to her, doing things back to him, no longer wanting me. But the other half experienced a sudden flash of realisation that I was free! What is sauce for the goose is sauce for the gander, therefore I was free to enjoy other women.

But ironically enough, it turned out that I couldn't get a woman! Not for ages and ages, and not for lack of trying either.

I had several farcical adventures, though it's hardly worth going into the full details I chatted up a woman in a cake shop who became highly indignant when I finally got round to asking her out. I actually made a date with a trim young librarian but she got cold feet at the last minute and locked herself in the loo, Library Staff for the use of. A blonde traffic warden I fancied just failed to turn up. A petrol pump attendant who appealed to me on account of the shiny PVC macs and high boots she wore was convinced I was joking and nothing I could say would un-convince her. It took months of ogling and flattery before I made it, with Helen Meade, as much to my surprise as hers.

Actually I only went for her because she talked so uninhibitedly about sex. "There's been no sex between Jim and me for a fortnight!" she'd say, or some such intimate revelation. She more or less hinted, even in Hilary's presence, that she was available. So I took her out.

Looking back on this affair I can see that neither of us got much out of it. We didn't even like each other! Yet I suppose we both regarded it as an opportunity of getting what we wanted. Now, I don't need to tell you what *I* wanted: the usual male requirement, a quick poke with no strings attached.

What she wanted was a little more complicated. It can probably best be described as a wish to be thought to be in the swim, not to be missing anything. Why, in this so-called permissive society, shouldn't she be enjoying the odd extra-marital frolic? Most of her friends seemed to be doing it.

She dropped hints about us here and there. Even her baby-sitter saw her go out, on foot, followed two minutes later by St. George in his chariot. The word got around, as she intended. But instead of it making her the envy of her friends some of them passed disparaging remarks concerning her choice of lover. From her own lips I heard this. One friend said I was "too sedate" for Helen; another actually had the audacity to refer to me as "a bit of an old fuddy-duddy"! So she didn't get what she wanted.

As for me, I didn't either. Regrettably, frustratingly, no oats. Only a quick and furtive feel. Wretchedly adolescent. And this only on alternate Friday nights! It shows how keen we were on each other, to meet only fortnightly.

She made it clear from the start that she had no intention of having intercourse with me, and yet it wasn't long before she let me do it to her orally. Sheer hair-splitting, as I told her. Or was it lack of contraceptive means? And this is the most annoying part: all the time I was doing it to her she was loving it, though pretending not to, pulling my hair out by the roots and screeching "You beast! Oh, you are a beast! You beast, you! Stop it, you beast! No, for God's sake, don't stop!" and so on, and yet the mean bitch wouldn't do a thing to me. Once I guided her hand on to it but she snatched it away, the selfish bitch!

After about six meetings she told me she couldn't go on seeing me, making the excuse that Jim was getting suspicious. The real reason, as I later discovered was that she'd found a more eligible lover, a beanpole of a chap with a beard and way-out shirts and gear, closer to her own age. So that was the end of that.

But at least on the strength of this brief association I was able to recruit her and Jim for the coven.

After Helen, I sank back into lethargy. I didn't seem to have the energy to try for any other women. I stayed in night after night after night. Music was my solace. In fact if it hadn't been for music I doubt if I'd have had anything to live for. Drink? Yes, I arranged for a weekly delivery of beer and got through three or four pints an evening. I was smoking nearly three ounces of tobacco a week, and trying brands which I'd always regarded as too expensive previously. Well, it was my money. Hilary didn't go short of housekeeping, and as a part-time teacher she was all right for pocket money. So I indulged myself a little with beer, tobacco and music.

I grew too lazy to practice my scales, arpeggios and studies, so consequently my keyboard progress slowed and I grew frustrated at being unable to play the things I really loved, the big Beethoven sonatas, the Chopin, the Scarlatti, the Couperin *Ordres*. I knew I'd never make a decent shot at the *Hammerklavier* even if I practiced for a dozen lifetimes! In fact my playing degenerated into fooling about, hamming-up popular melodies from musicals and suchlike, or wallowing in clumsy and cacophonous improvisation.

Apart from that I spent hours every evening listening to recordings. I joined a Music Club which as well as lending gave me the option of buying disc at reduced prices.

The Brandenburgs, the Forty-Eight, Vivaldi, the Mahler and Bruckner symphonies, the Schubert chamber works, were more than merely an escape from a boring and trivial everyday world. They were a reality in themselves; a perfect, heightened, untarnishable reality. As soon as I got myself settled in the lounge in the evenings I was up and away into this magical music-world. My impeccable guides were men like Rubinstein and Brendel, von Karajan and Klemperer, Fischer-Dieskau and the Amadeus. I worshipped their very names. I devoutly read each page of the monthly *Gramophone;* it was the missal to my music-religion.

"Has anybody told you what a mess you look, these days?" asked Hilary one evening. I frowned. I had a historic disc of Schnabel playing the Opus 110 sonata on the turntable and hardly welcomed her intrusion. She stood by the door, wearing eye-shadow, an innovation for her, and smelling like a chemist's shop. She was looking down on me pityingly.

"What do you mean by that?" I growled.

"I mean that you look perfectly horrible, most unappetising," she said.

"Balls," I replied. "I wouldn't want to be eaten by *you,* anyway."

"There's no chance of your being eaten by anybody, believe me!. No woman in her right mind could possibly fancy you. Just look at you! Ash all down your cardigan, reeking of booze and that foul pipe, revolting breath, horrible paunch. Ugh! I can't stand the sight of you! I'm going."

"Well, go!" I said after her as she banged the lounge door. "Stand not upon the order of your going, but in the words of the immortal bard, bugger off!" I felt most peeved at having my concert ruined like that. I put the disc on again at the start. Schnabel deserved a fresh hearing after being tainted by such cheap feminine bitchiness. As far as my own person went, perhaps she was right. I did look a bit of a slob. But on the inside of me, inside my mind, inside my soul, I was one of the elect. As soon as I heard the opening bars of a work I was up there with the immortal ones.

The first flush of my love affair with music lasted about the same length of time as my love for Hilary, that is, about two years. Then it began to decline. The repertoire of works to be explored, the list of composers to be sampled, seemed at first inexhaustible. But eventually I reached a point where I could hardly find any more of my kind of music, of the music with just that special flavour that could make the hairs prickle on my scalp or bring those mysterious strange stirrings or even a sudden flood of tears. I turned to score-reading as a shot in the arm. But gradually I became a technical connoisseur and cataloguer rather than a true lover of music. The thrills became rarer and rarer. Re-hearings of once-loved works brought an odd kind of depression.

I drank more, smoked more, listened less, and even began to watch a lot of television, though I'd always formerly despised it and been loud in my denunciations of it.

The evenings were no longer magical. After my day's teaching I would plough through my dinner mechanically, though Hilary had always been a good cook, and apathetically slide into the land of pipe, slippers and booze. I was less than half alive. I had not the faintest flicker of interest in anything.

It therefore came as something of a shock when I encountered something that stirred my curiosity. Of all things a documentary on the television.

27

Chapter 3

I WAS sitting slumped in front of it, the television that is. The sound was low. I've always hated the way people have it turned up as if they're deaf. I was vaguely aware of faces and hands moving on the screen, mouths opening and shutting, but I wasn't paying much attention. Instead, I found myself doing a vague semi-conscious kind of stocktaking. My pipe kept going out. Packed too tight. I observed that one of my slippers had a hole in the toe. My top two trouser buttons were undone on account of an enormous pie and chips for dinner. My beer glass was nearly empty. Too late to go round to the off-licence for a fresh supply. I belched, but without real satisfaction.

It was true, I realised. I *was* a slob. Hilary's remarks about my unappetising-ness were quite justified. Not that I really wanted any woman to fancy me. I had a pretty poor opinion of women on the whole: their falseness, from false tits to false sentiments, their over-sweet smell, their selfish grasping materialistic bitchiness, made me want to puke. By the way, don't think from this that I'm gay. I certainly didn't fancy men, either. But at least there was something *noble* in man. It was man and not woman who produced the Last Judgement, the Eroica, the Gormanghast trilogy. Women's minds are so bound up with the trivial. No depth to them, no vision. Or so I thought, at this, the lowest ebb of my life.

And even though I might be a slob, I consoled myself, I had vision. Although, was this still true? Should I not say that I used to have vision? I'd sunk down into the mire lately, no two ways about it. I'd sunk to the level of watching this muck, for instance.

I glared morosely at the screen. A western. A sentimental western. The hero. A young man of incredibly lean jaw and clean morals, leans

28

from the rail of the guard's van. He waves his stetson in farewell to a conventionally beautiful girl in puffy sleeves whose heart he has won but whom he must leave in order to stir another of the fair sex, in the next gripping instalment.

Like many viewers I hadn't the strength to switch off, hoping there'd be 'something better on next'. I could hardly know, at that moment, that the next programme would change the course of my life. And even while it was on I didn't realise its importance. It was only afterwards that I found I couldn't stop thinking about it.

It was a documentary, so-called, on Witchcraft.

As soon as I heard the opening announcement I said to myself Oh yes? Here we go. Another lot of old codswallop! Broadly, the programme was divided into three parts: first, a number of interviews with men and women who said they were practising members of "the Craft", as they called it; secondly, a monologue by a self-styled Arch High-priest; and, thirdly, film of a coven at work. I felt my lips curling in a sceptical sneer throughout. The interviewees, though earnest, were bumbling and inarticulate, unable to convey exactly what it was that appealed to them about their cult. They were neither working class nor upper crust. Though fairly bright I would not have called them intellectuals. White-collar and minor professions would probably be nearer the mark. The only thing that came over was their keenness. The High-priest was a way-out character who made several extravagant claims, such as the grovelling obedience of covens up and down the country, or the power to kill a man with a word. His wild staring eyes supported his claims, but his weak mouth and puny physique belied them. I thought the last part was the best. Clever camera work and the choice of setting, a ruined chapel, combined to evoke a dark and dramatic atmosphere. A simplified rite of Initiation was performed. Only the dancing spoiled it, a ludicrous note being struck by the elephantine buttocks of the women and bellies of the men. None but the lithe and lissome should cavort in the nude, I reflected. Which certainly left me out! The programme ended with the statement that this was the fastest-growing social phenomenon in Britain today, and

29

that 'unknown to you, your ordinary-seeming neighbours may be witches.' Pan down to flickering flames, swell of eerie music, cymbals, hands raised in supplication, picture of horned god, sunrise over ancient stone circle. Finis. I switched off and stumbled into the kitchen to make myself a cup of coffee. Didn't give it another thought until the following evening.

Hilary and I were having a late tea. For once she was not going out.

"Do you know anything about witchcraft?" I asked. Not that I really expected her to, but it was simply that I could hear the television blathering away to itself in the lounge and was reminded of what I'd seen the previous evening.

"No," she replied. And then, after a pause, "but I think it's very interesting."

"Do you? Do you really?" I exclaimed. "I'm surprised. I shouldn't have thought you'd have had any time for it at all."

"Oh, I think it's a fascinating subject."

"Ah, subject. I see. You mean fascinating to read about?"

"Yes. What else do you think I mean?"

"You mean you'd like reading about it, but you wouldn't actually, you know, wish to take part?"

"No, I certainly would not. I should think it'd be highly dangerous to dabble in things like that."

"Oh, yes. It would, indeed. Quite agree."

Much later, about ten-thirty, I was rather surprised to hear myself saying, apropos of nothing, "You know what a coven is, don't you?"

"You're not still on about that, are you?"

"Yes. *Do* you know what a coven is?"

"Well, it's thirteen people, isn't it?"

"Doesn't have to be. The full coven is. But a small coven can consist of only three or four."

"Really?"

"Yes (pause) I tell you what – let's start a coven."

Chapter 4

BUT, as I might have known, she wouldn't. If I was going to start a coven I'd have to do it on my own.

Was it a whim? Did I seriously want to become a witch? Or, was it a warlock? The idea certainly intrigued me. Several days later it still intrigued me. I'd been thinking about it on and off practically all the time. But I realised I knew damn-all about the subject. Obviously the first thing to do was to bone up on it.

After lingering about with my coat collar turned up against a blustery wind, on the Tuesday of the following week, it was with relief that I saw the Staffordshire County Libraries' mobile van arrive. I'd patronised it just once before and I didn't hold out any great hopes.

I asked the young lady librarian if she had a Dewey Classification list and, after some searching, she produced a copy which looked as if it could have been contemporary with Dewey himself. Witchcraft and Magic, I noted, was classified under category 133.0, Secret Societies under 366.0 and Comparative Religion under 294.0.

The library van was rather like Dr. Who's *Tardis*. It seemed much larger inside than one would guess from the outside. The counter was down at the front end, backing on to the driver's cab, and along the considerable length of the van were rows of compact shelving and occasional revolving display stands for paperbacks. Regrettably, it seemed to carry mainly Fiction, Children's Fiction and a few items of Biography. Reference books were scarce.

The only volume I could find of interest to me was a popular paperback. It was a potted history of witches, their alleged doings, persecution of same via the edict *Malleus Maleficarum,* and tales of the pitiless Witchfinder-General, Matthew Hopkins. I skimmed it rapidly.

The author admitted to having had no practical experience. His tone was dismissive. Quite useless.

I decided to try my luck in the local metropolis, Lichfield.

The Lichfield Public Library is housed in a good-sized building, formerly the College of Art. Its high ceilings and many windows make it a light and airy place, But to my mind it lacks atmosphere.

I remember being told that the library was at one time situated in a much older building on Beacon Street, at the edge of the park. One of the earliest free lending libraries in England, I owed its existence to the generosity of Andrew Carnegie. More architecturally interesting, with its hexagonal tower and blind Romanesque arcading, it had been deemed inadequate.

The only consolation for my leanings towards the ancient and romantic was to be enjoyed at the new library's entrance. A yew-shaded drive curves across in front of a sturdy house, the only building to survive Henry VIII's *Dissolution,* and once the home of George (or, was it Gregory?) Stonynge, Guild Master and Bailiff of the City. It was made of the same warm, weathered, rich red sandstone of the old Friary ruins across the road, and indeed of the cathedral itself.

But, to business. I was allowed access to a modern computerised version of the old Whitaker's *British Books in Print* and from this I noted down a few promising titles.

To avoid frequent trips to Lichfield, I filled in request slips at the mobile library van, the next time it came to the village.

The books were so long arriving, more than four weeks, that I got quite annoyed. As a Council Tax payer, I deserved better service.

The first things I read were the standard 'classics': Gerald Gardner, Montague Summers, Margaret Murray. Then I was lucky enough to borrow, through an ex-colleague of mine who was now in Further Education, bound volumes of the magazine *Man, Myth and Magic,* in which I found articles on modern witchcraft. Much more to my liking. And then, better still, I dropped on the very thing I was looking for, in a Birmingham bookshop: a newly-published book, entirely about pressent-day witches. After thumbing it through I bought it, despite the off-putting price.

Ah, this was the real McCoy! Detailed eye-witness accounts of initiation ceremonies, casting of spells, calling up of spirits, raising of the cone of power – basic rituals with full particulars of essential words and actions. Fascinating! I gobbled it up.

Armed with my new knowledge I was raring to go. Which should it be? Join a coven? Or start one?

In the end I decided to join a coven first to gain practical experience.

How exactly does one set about finding a coven? Witches don't seek you out. You have to seek *them*. But how? They're not in Yellow Pages, under W. They have no fixed premises. They don't advertise.

Ah, now there was an idea. Even though *they* don't advertise, there was no reason why I shouldn't.

I cut out the form from the back of a weekly advertisement paper, one which I noted had a wide circulation in the Midlands and an extensive Personal column, and filled it in:

Gentleman, 39, wishes to contact practising students of Wicca.

Box number required (naturally!) There we are. I had my doubts as to whether gentlemanliness mattered, but the wording was at least concise, veiled as far as the layman was concerned, and discreet-sounding. I sent it off with a cheque to cover cost including the forwarding of replies to me.

I waited. One week, two weeks. Damn-all! No, I wasn't going to get any replies. But I suppose I shouldn't have expected any. People involved in witchcraft would hardly spend their time scanning the *cris de coeur* of Widower, 60, clean and respectable. Or Divorcee, 32, seeks friendship, view marriage, in the hope of finding somebody who wants to be a witch!

But one morning Hilary handed me a buff envelope. I slipped upstairs without offering any explanation, to open it.

33

Dear Sir (it said)

I am writing because I saw your advertisment (wrong spelling, I noted, with a teacher's unerring eye). My friend and I are both of the Old Religion. We are students of it also as you mention.

Would you write to us and then peraps you might visit us?

I'm afraid to say we have not had a meeting for a long time but we have been in corespondance with another follower of the Old Religion and hope to asemble soon.

Flags Flax Fodder and Frigg
Blessed Be.

Peter Quince

The heading bore the date of the previous day and a Wolverhampton address. I looked it up in my A-Z. A poor district, judging by the closeness of the streets, certainly terraced houses if not back-to-backs.

An odd letter, to say the least. Who were these characters mentioned at the end? Flags, Flax and so on? Possibly deities. Perhaps the writer was saying "In the name of," these? Peter Quince was the carpenter in *A Midsummer Night's Dream*. But of course if the chap, whoever he was, preferred to use a pseudonym, that was his business.

The tone of the letter? Not exactly literate. The mis-spellings of advertisement, and other words,'correspondence', 'assemble', together with a rather naïve kind of phrasing. I didn't know what to think.

I realised that I had subconsciously been hoping for an address in Solihull or Four Oaks, or somewhere like that. At the back of my mind - I confess – there must have been a vision of bored housewives of the rather sophisticated professional and executive class displaying their pampered charms in the buff. What a dirty old sod I must be! And a snobbish one, too, you might say. But this was not a matter of pure snobbery. People of one's own class or slightly above would almost certainly be bound to be more discreet. Like oneself they would have something to lose. Also there was the point that a smart address would suggest something attractive and well-groomed. Whereas – Sebastopol

34

Street! Something slatternly and greasy? Quite probable.

There was only one way to find out.

Hilary went out at about 7.l5   (It was   either Ron or Alfie, but naturally she wouldn't bother to tell me.) As soon as she'd gone I fetched the letter from under a pile of magazines in the bottom of my wardrobe and got out my pen and some notepaper.

Dear Peter Quince (I wrote, after a moment's thought)
Thank you very much for your letter.

I must explain at the outset that I have never been a member of a coven and that my interest in the Craft so far has been purely theoretical. I have read books by a number of standard authorities such as Dr. Gerald Gardner and I am keen to meet people with the same interest.

The reason for this (I thought I'd better convince Quince – forgive me – of my good intentions, lest he should think I'm out for kinky thrills, which of course I am!) is bound up with my view of the nature of modern life and with my reactions to it. I'd say that our supermarket-cum-television culture is one that effectively blinds us to our deeper levels of understanding, to our possibilities of spiritual awareness, and to our essential qualities and potentialities as human beings (I do in fact believe this). And I would think that those people who study and engage in psychic or occult activity are amongst the few who can be said to be truly alive. It is ironic that they are so often maligned or mis-represented luridly in the gutter press.

Please understand that I am a seeker after truth and a person who wishes to live at a deeper level than mere materialism. I should admit that I am owed some of these ideas, particularly about 'deeper levels' and 'potentiality', to Colin Wilson's brilliant 600-page study *The Occult.*

I have a car and would be glad to come and visit you, if you will give me a date and time when this would be convenient.

Yours sincerely,
George Whitehouse.

I addressed an envelope, found a stamp, and having re-read the letter before sealing it, put it on the dining-room table. Then I went upstairs to get a jacket and shoes.

I'd no sooner opened my wardrobe than I heard a key turn in the front door. I came downstairs to find Hilary at the sideboard drawer.

"I left my keys. My car keys I mean – and I'll need it after all," she explained.

"Really? Nothing wrong with Alfie's car is there?"

"None of your business! I never mentioned Alfie. And I must get off now. I'm in a hurry. Do you want me to post this for you?" She picked up my letter from the table.

"No, no, not at all," I said hastily. "As a matter of fact I was just going out for a breath of air. I'll post it myself."

"Hmmm. Peter Quince? Who's he?"

"Oh, nobody. Just a colleague. Secretary of a study group I'm involved with. Literature in Primary Schools. Questionnaire you know."

"Fascinating, I'm sure. Sounds like quince jam to me."

"Ah, jam. Yes, exactly. As a matter of fact he is in jam, young Quince. Very old jam family. In on the ground floor with Golliwog, if you"ll forgive the racist expression." I looked at her through half-closed eyes, rather pleased with my inventiveness, but wondering if I'd taken it too far.

"I'm off," she announced decisively. "Haven't time to stand around listening to a lot of nonsense about jam!"

"You started it," I said mildly.

"Oh, of course! Naturally! *I* always start *everything*. Always have done!" she snapped, and flounced out. I picked up the letter and placed it carefully in my breast pocket. I gave her five minutes and then strolled down to the post box.

Peter Quince replied by return. Wednesday evening was all right, he said, any time after seven.

Wednesday came. I wasn't sure what to wear. Sounds a bit

36

womanish, but it's a practical point. How should one dress to go and meet witches? Natty suit? Sweater and old cords? No doubt a black robe with mystic designs would be the ideal, but in lieu of that I put on a sports jacket and flannels.

Route finding was not one of my strong points. By the time I had driven south through Rugeley and Cannock, crossed the M6 and M54 motorways, and passed through Bushbury into increasingly built-up areas, I began to feel uncertain.

When I entered the maze of small streets encircled by Wolverhampton's ring road, I soon became lost. This despite the recent purchase of my A-Z Street Atlas.

Then, by luck, I found it. Sebastopol Street. Its name gave some indication of its age. Crimean war period. Its houses looked uniformly poky and grimy. It was the sort of street where you would be uneasy about leaving your car unattended I coasted along until I found number 14. Why on earth do they make house numbers so hard to spot? After locking up carefully I mounted an unswept flight of stone stairs leading to a door with stained glass panels. There were three bell-pushes with faded yellow name cards behind plastic. None of them said Peter Quince. But then why should they? As there was 14, 14A and 14B I thought I'd better ring plain No. 14. I rang

If I'd expected some swinging young mini-skirted witch, or even a wrinkled crone attended by familiars, then I'd have been disappointed. The person who in fact answered the door was a tallish, leanish, greyish man of about fifty-five to sixty. We looked at each other expectantly.

"Good evening. My name's George Whitehouse." I said at length, and was rather annoyed to hear myself sounding like a television compere.

"Yes?" said the man.

"I, er, would you happen to be Mr. Quince? Er, that is, Peter Quince?"

"Tom Tydeman," he said, shaking his head mournfully. "No Quince. No such person as Quince."

"Then I've come to the wrong – "

37

"No. No, not at all. We've been expecting you. Come in. And I'll explain the er, er-hurmm... Do come this way."

I followed him down a narrow dark hall filled with cooking smells, into a kind of kitchen-cum-dining room. The place was unbelievably cluttered. It was one of those places which seem bunged up to the ceiling with fusty old furniture and assorted junk, and yet the details are beyond recall. I had a claustrophobic feeling, increased by the heat from a two-bar electric fire.

A grey-haired lady in a grey cashmere cardigan rose from her armchair to greet me.

"Mr. Whitehouse," announced Tom Tydeman.

"How nice to see you," croaked. She looked thin and bird-like, and the hand she extended to me was bony and purple-veined. "I am Peter Quince," she said, "at any rate for the purpose of occult correspondence. You see, it's useful. Whenever Tom gets a letter addressed to 'Peter' we know straight away that it's for me. I don't live here, you see. I merely use Tom as an address. You see?"

"Yes, yes, of course," I said. In my bewilderment I'd been unconsciously picking at the tasselled end of a table runner. Tom gently disengaged my hand from it and ushered me into a chair.

'Peter' leaned forward a little and focussed her tired grey eyes on mine. I noticed a shelf behind her, crowded with chemist's jars, each jar containing brownish dried matter, herbs I guessed. I blew my nose discreetly into my handkerchief, and turned my attention to Peter again. She leaned forward until I thought she was going to overbalance on to my knees.

"Marsh-mallow?" she croaked. By the interrogative tone I took this for an invite to refreshments.

"No, thank you all the same. I've not long had a meal."

"Makes no difference. Quite all right after meals. After, or before. No difference." This sounded very odd, but I didn't feel inclined to discuss the wisdom of Peter's eating habits.

"Have some," she said dramatically, startling me. I blinked, but

38

before I could refuse she'd produced a jar from beside her chair, unstoppered it and handed it to me together with a small spoon.

"What, er, what is it?" I asked foolishly. Odd odour. I wasn't keen at all.

"Marsh-mallow. Said so, didn't I? Very good, very very good indeed. Just the thing for *your* complaint. Highly soothing to the mucous membrane. (Hm – spotted that I was a catarrh sufferer, eh? Even though I wasn't troubled by it at the moment.) Soothes away all your irritation. Might tell you, Mr. Whitehouse, once upon a time people knew the value of the Old Remedies. Days gone by – 'fore folk put their faith in pills and disgusting muck out of needles – your humble Marsh-mallow was the cure-all. Cures most things, Mr. Whitehouse. Cures most things, even today, I'll tell you."

I boggled. My head was spinning. And when I took a deep breath to try and clear it another smell filled my nostrils and made me wrinkle up my nose.

"Field penny cress," supplied Peter. "Used to go by the name of Mithridate Mustard. Just boiling some up in the kitchen. You should always have a bit by you. Antidote to poisons, you see."

"Yes, I saw. Or rather I smelled. Peter went on talking but I wasn't listening. I kept asking myself, "What the hell am I doing here?" and telling myself that if I stayed much longer I'd become nutty as my hosts! Peter broke in on my reflections:

Have to do me cooking in here, you see. Won't allow it in the Home. Made me take all me jars out of me room. Can't do anything there in that dratted place. They'll be sorry, though. No mustard. You see?"

Tom tapped me on the forearm. "Mithridate Mustard, her means. Antidote, remember?" *She's* got the wort-cunning. They haven't. See? I shook my head. Tom gave me a long-suffering look and spelled it out: "Setterwort in the soup, marsh-marigold buds instead of capers. Could be quite safe, but only if you pickle 'em. Got to have the cunning. Otherwise, could be nasty."

"But, er, doesn't Peter eat anything at the Home?"

"Does, 'course she does. But she's got the cunning!"

39

"Cunning?" They both gave me withering looks, as if I were an imbecile child.

I had the feeling that if *they* were not quite what I was looking for, then *I* was certainly not what they were looking for!

"Be done by now," said Peter. "Come along, Mr. Whitehouse. See how Tom's fixed me up." I followed her into the kitchen.

There were two shelves beside the cooker, both of them groaning under the weight of assorted vessels of earthenware, crock, glass, even china, anything but plastics, all doubtless containing virulent poisons. And antidotes, of course.

Peter removed an old-fashioned two-handled saucepan from the gas and poured its contents through a strainer into a bowl.

"Like me cauldron, eh? Womb of Nature, you see. The Magic's conceived in it."

She began to take jars down from the shelves, one by one, and made me sniff them.

"Fumitory," she croaked, "efficacious in every case, Mr. Whitehouse. Then there's your Lady's Bedstraw – curdles milk, or you can make it into a strong dye. Your Common Fleabane – for dysentery. Coltsfoot – for your chesty coughs. Henbane – not just a poison as folk think, but cures horses. And then there's your Prunella Vulgaris – Self-heal to the layman, or if you like your actual Carpenter's Herb, your Hook-head, Sickle-wort, or just plain Prunella – cures for any wound, inward or outward. You see, Mr. Whitehouse?
You see?"

No, I didn't. Not really. But what I did see was that I had to get the hell out of there before I went cuckoo!

"I, er, look here, this is most interesting. Er, fascinating, absolutely. But as a matter of fact I do happen to have another appointment. In fact I'm due at the house of a solicitor friend of mine at, er, (surreptitious glance at wrist watch: five past nine) at ...Oh my God! Nine o'clock! Should've been there already. I'm going to be rather late. Sorry to have to dash off."

I was wasting my breath, though. She wasn't listening. "When's your birthday, then?" she asked.

"M - May the 30th," I faltered.

"Ah, you're a Gemini. I knew it. Soon as I saw you! Well, if you look on my Flora Chart you'll see what's yours. (She pointed to a card hanging above the cooker. It had a design of a circle divided into twelve sectors, one for each sign of the zodiac.) I've no need to look meeself, of course. If you're a Gemini your blossoms'll be snapdragon, filbert and elder."

"Oh."

"Yes, I can see you're a Gemini. There's a time for collecting, you know."

"Ah, collecting."

You have to harvest your herbs at the right phase of the moon. Waxing moon to build, waning to destroy, though we don't do much of that, do we, Tom?" Tom shook his head gravely.

It's very interesting, all of it, I must say," I mumbled, "but, I really must…"

"Not at all, not at all. You should take a drink with us before you go, Mr. Whitehouse," said Tom. "Peter brews a lovely cordial. Better than anything you'd get in your wine shops. A spot of our Fumitory Elixir will put you on top of the world."

Or six feet under it, I told myself. I said it was imperative that I leave at once, and placated them with the promise of a further visit. At length Tom reluctantly led the way to the front door, while Peter returned to her concoctions.

As I stumbled down the steps and unlocked the door of my car I gulped lungfuls of air. I thought it had never smelled so sweet.

Chapter 5

MY next contact with the witchy people was just as peculiar but very different. In a way it was quite beautiful. Poetic, even moving, if you go for that sort of thing.

It was also extremely confusing. So much so that I doubt if I could tell you what happened. In my own words, that is. So I'll have to use somebody else's.

I'm going to quote from a Report written by a member of the group, Simon Chubb, and printed in a litho magazine, a copy of which Simon later posted to me. Here it is, then. Interpolations in brackets by yours truly.

'I approached this, my first pagan Rite, with some trepidation (wrote Simon). I was full of enthusiasm, but doubtful as to whether I would be able to make any real contribution. But my friendship with Mick Melly was a reassuring factor. I knew he'd organise things well and inspire us all. Therefore I expected everything to go perfectly smoothly.

But it didn't.

I arrived at *Withywindle,* Mick's house on the fringes of Cannock Chase, on a Friday afternoon to find him and Pam talking to two would-be gatecrashers! Their names, I learned, were Kate Steinweg and Cy Clark. Cy was a young fresh-faced girl and Kate a sweet woman in her late twenties. Liz was in hospital, I was told. This was the first of our misfortunes, the loss of our hostess and culinary expert.

The whole of Saturday was spent in shuttling back and forth fetching people from far and wide, with only two cars available.

The afternoon brought us another gatecrasher (Pssst! Yours truly – George Whitehouse Esq!) who proved to be an educated person (hem,

42

hem) and – so we believed at first – a sincere and devout follower of the Pagan Movement, though we were later to change our opinion.

In the evening we began our discussion. Ted Pullman skilfully conducted, guided and summarised a debate between seventeen people! The difficulty of routing out suitable apparatus and robes for all, combined with the cold, wetness and cloud, at first threatened to dispirit us. But as we read through Frank Fielding's transcription of the Goddess's myth we became inspired. And I was not the only newcomer to make enthusiastic suggestions. (Even gorgeous George made one or two. But hardly the kind that he really had in mind).

Kate, Cy and Oliver were chosen to take the parts of Wlwa, Miriel and Lamba, and though these first two were absolute novices an unexpected beauty was made manifest through their renderings. (Quite agree. Bedworthy, both of them.) If we had had our doubts at first about their commitment, these were quickly dispelled.

Earlier, a group of us had chosen a place for the Rite, and had built a fire in a circle of thirteen stones. It was a delightful spot, hidden in the vastness of Cannock Chase, on rising ground to the east of Sherbrook Valley.

Not far below us the southern stepping-stones afforded a dry-shod passage across the brook. Less well known than their counterparts to the north, which had a picnic site nearby, much visited in the summer months, these stones were the marker for members of our group. All they had to do was walk uphill, eastwards, until they came to it: our special glade.

Mick and Pam had found it on one of their walks. With two more of our dedicated followers they carried white stones up from the water's edge, blessing each of them as they were ritually laid in a circle beneath the trees. On their arrival at the spot three pigeons had flown up. The omens were propitious!

We set out from *Withywindle* for the glade at midnight, and immediately a heart-warming togetherness sprang up amongst us. (Not true: I took Cy's hand, but she wouldn't play.) Those present were: my good friend Mick Melly, Kate Steinweg – who was to play Wlwa,

Cy Clark – Miriel, Oliver Malley – Lemba, Frank Fielding – Tor, Pam Doone – Aiwa, and also Tim Burke, Petrena Howth, Mike Howth, Ted Pullman, Pete Copley, Dick Orange, Debbie Smith, Tina Jacobs, Jack Turner, our third gatecrasher whose name, if I've got it right, was George Whitehouse (you have – it is) and finally myself, Simon Chubb.

We entered the stone circle and linked hands, only too painfully aware that we'd been hasty and far from thorough in our preparations. Pamela invoked the Goddess, asking her blessing, asking her to raise and transmute our Rite from the level of mere mumming to a thing transcendent. We went to appointed positions outside the stone circle, those who were to represent the gods moving apart from the rest.

Then we others, humble acolytes, saw a flickering luminosity. Two torches glowed and drew near. Dick Orange began to beat the drum – we had improvised by using a plastic dustbin, up turned – and it sounded like the throb of a mighty heart beating. We softly called the Mother by her sacred name: "Wlwa... Wlwa... Wlwa " keeping time with the drum as the lights drew ever closer. The Goddess came. In love she came. (I could say something, but I'll resist it). In love she heard our supplication, heard and warmly took our prayer to her bosom.

Suddenly the three stood before us: Wlwa, Miriel and Aiwa. From Miriel's neck there hung down upon her breast the fragrant garland of meadowsweet woven for her by the tender hands of Cy. There with them, slightly to the rear, stood the hag, cloaked and hooded.

Wlwa gave life and birth to Lemba and Tor. They arose. Miriel held out here flame to us as she passed *deasil* around the circle. Lemba with his recorder followed in her footsteps making a soft plaintive tune. Then Aiwa took Miriel's torch and extinguished its light. In the dark she circled, *widdershins,* a cold shadow, menacing and traceable only by the faint light which she carried. (A bike lamp wrapped in a yellow nylon underslip, actually. G.) But her light went out and a fresh torch of oil-soaked rag had to be kindled for her. Yet we were not dismayed. Her loving arms enfolded us. We were her children.

Regretfully, at this juncture, our third gatecrasher, George, lowered the tone of the proceedings by his unseemly behaviour, a form of

44

behaviour highly irreverent to the Goddess. (Nonsense – it was no more than a genteel feel!) He was, after all, not one of us. Duly he was rebuked, and calm was restored.

Then, in spite of earlier cloudiness, the moon revealed herself in all her glory, lending her concern and blessing upon our Rite.

Wlwa gave her light to Tor, and he lit the fire we had built. But alas the branches were damp and too green and would not light. Yet no blame was proffered, no loss of confidence could now assail us. We were moved and comforted by an indescribable wave of joy.

We stood before the Goddess in an arc. She blessed water and apples and we partook of them. "Welcome my child, to this feast," she greeted each one of us. She put our hands in Miriel's and she caressed us while we knelt for the kiss of the maid. She gave us water and rebuked Aiwa who would have denied us. She gave us each an apple, with love.

Then the Goddess who had blessed us by the warmth of her presence, departed. We held hands and called down blessings upon all Pagans wherever they might be. Nine times we danced around the circle. We threw our hair loose and laughed and raised our faces to the moon. We knelt to kiss the earth, and knew the Great Love. Strangers, we had come together to honour the Old Religion. Together we had found beauty, fear, power, gentleness, ecstasy! We were all one in the Mother!

Simon Chubb'

Well, perhaps they <u>had</u> found something, the faery people. But I hadn't.

45

Chapter 6

LETTERS to sources mentioned in Simon Chubb's magazine led me to ... to what? Yes, I'm afraid so – to another group of the faery people. Also to a pair of astrologers, and to a large medium lady. Or should I say a medium-large lady? She was at least that, judging by the photo she sent me along with half a ream of good advice.

No use. No use whatsoever. I only got as far as corresponding with them, but they were clearly not what I was after.

Oddly enough, I met my first dedicated witch in the mobile library van.

I was standing in the narrow space at the counter waiting to have my books stamped, and, why not admit it, trying to look down the young lady librarian's blouse while I waited, when I became aware of a woman at my elbow. The first thing I noticed was her smell. Imagine, if you can, with your nose, a god-awful mixture of cheap scents. Californian Poppy, Ashes of Dustbin, Eau de Closet. Add a strong dash of musk and joss sticks, and you might get an idea of it.

I turned and saw her, and the expression 'mutton dressed up as lamb' immediately sprang to mind. Her black-dyed hair was tightly curled, with ringlets hanging down beside cheeks plastered with rouge. Her lipstick was deep carmine, her eyes were black pebbles. The wrinkles at her throat were partly hidden by an orange chiffon scarf held by a silver ring. She wore a white clinging jumper, a much-too-short tight black skirt, and a pair of white boots of the soft plastic type which pull up to the knee, and look all right until they start to slip and wrinkle, which hers did. Her knees were dimpled.

"It's a good one, that is, " she said, pointing to one of my books. It had a lurid cover, showing a naked girl being used as an altar during an

46

occult ritual and bearing the title *Present-day Witchcraft Practices in England.*

I looked at her carefully. Fifty-plus, I'd say. Heavy make-up. Hoarse voice. What my late mother would have called 'a bit on the common side', to put it mildly!

"Oh, is it? Good," I murmured, with studied vagueness.

Just then a second young lady librarian left off what she was doing and stamped the woman's books. She finished in a dead heat with the one who was stamping mine. I caught a glimpse of a ticket: Upton, Agnes (Mrs), 40 Shrewsbury Avenue. Ah, a neighbour. Well almost. Shrewsbury was next to Horton Drive where I lived.

"Read a lot of these books, do you?" asked Mrs. Upton, as she shuffled her choice into her shopping bag. They were, I noticed, *Witchfinder General* by Ronald Bassett and *The Silver Chalice* by Thomas B. Costain.

"Well, I wouldn't say a lot," I replied, packing mine into my briefcase. "It's quite an interesting subject."

"Interesting? Fascinatin' , you mean! It's the most fascinatin' subjeck in the whole world!" she exclaimed. Her speech and looks were such that I expected her to add 'dearie' on to everything she said, like a tart in a novel, but she didn't. "When you really get to know it, that is," she added, hinting at a long experience of witchery.

"Have you read a lot of this, er, kind of book yourself, Mrs. Upton," I countered.

"Owja know my name?" she asked.

"I saw it on your library ticket just a moment ago," I said. By this time we were on our way out. I glanced back to see the librarians following us with their eyes, no doubt thinking us a proper pair of freaks. I held the door open and Mrs. Upton passed through.

"That your car?" she asked.

"Yes. I'll give you a lift if you like."

"Thank you very much," she said, and climbed awkwardly into the passenger seat, showing an unnecessary amount of leg. What she showed, I must admit, was surprisingly good for her age.

47

"Yes, I read a lot," she said as we moved off. "Got a lot of books of my own. On that *subjeck*, you know. 'Smatter of fact you could borrow one or two, if I could be sure you'd return 'em all right?"

"Oh, of course. You can trust me with books, Mrs. Upton. Ought to know how to take care of them, being a teacher."

"Teacher? What's your name?"

"Whitehouse. George Whitehouse."

"Should've known it! You teach in the village school. Our Jenny's Wayne says you 'hit him'.

"Your Jenny's Wayne?"

"My daughter's lad Wayne Smirke, 'is name is. Only in the Infants. But he says you hit him."

"Impossible," I said dismissively. An image popped up of a scruffy, snotty-nosed little brat whose hand I'd smacked in the dining hall for going round the tables salting everybody's water. "Impossible," I repeated. "It's against the Council's ruling on Corporal Punishment. He was probably, ahem, confusing me with Mr. Owen." Rat that I was, trying to drop poor old Gareth in it.

"Oh well, can't say as I'd blame you if you did thump 'is earhole. He can be a right little barstid when he likes! Ah, here we are, then. You pop round later on, Mr. Whitehouse, and I'll look you out some of them books. Or I'll bring 'em round *to you*, if you tell me your number?"

"No, er, no, it would be better if *I* came round to *you*," I put in hastily.

"As you like it. I'll expect you, then."

"Yes. Thanks a lot."

"Don't mention it. Thank *you*. For the ride I mean." I watched her hobble down her drive, exaggeratedly swaying her buttocks, as I reversed and made a turn in the road.

This is my daughter, Jenny. Oh, sit down Mr. Whitehouse. Here, by me. You know Mr. Whitehouse, don't you Jenny?"

"Yiss. I know 'im. 'E 'it my Wayne in school, 'e did!" I looked at Jenny. Recognized her at once. Ought to, as she lives less than a dozen houses away from me and traipses up and down the road umpteen times a day, dragging snotty Wayne with her. She's about twenty-six, slim, leggy, fairish hair. She was wearing her usual get-up of catskin coat, wool mini-dress with a belt of gold rings, and the inevitable white plastic pull-up boots. I remonstrated with her, in a manner that was intended to sound jocular and soothing: "Come, come, Mrs. Smirke. Wouldn't dream of doing such a thing. As I was saying to your mother, the boy must have confused me with Mr. Owen."

"Oh, no 'e didn't! 'E were quite positive. The fat one, 'e said."

Fat one, indeed! I may have acquired a slight suggestion of a beer pot but I've not got as much paunch as Gareth Owen!

"Well, that clinches it," I said, like a character in a TV western.. "Mr. Owen's certainly fatter than me. Must've been him."

"With glasses, our Wayne said. The fat one with glasses. And Mr. Owen don't wear no glasses, so it must've bin you!"

"Jenny, Jenny! Don't go on at Mr. Whitehouse like that, love. Here, listen, he's one of us."

"One of us?"

"You know. The Craft, love. I asked him round to see the books. I'm lending him a few of them. He's very interested, he says."

"Yes, yes, I am!" I put in, seizing the opportunity to steer the talk away from the subject of Wayne. "In fact I've read quite a few books about witchcraft already."

"*The Craft*, dear. Just, *The Craft,*" said Mrs. Upton.

"Indeed . The Craft." I smiled my gratitude to her for putting me wise as to the correct terminology, and went on: "Yes, I think I've read most of the usual ones: Margaret Murray, Montague Summers, Gerald Gardner."

"I don't know about them first two you mentioned, but Dr. Gardner,'e was a good 'un. We've been to 'is museum, Jenny and me. Castletown, Isle of Man. Some very interesting things there, ain't there, Jen?"

"Yiss, Mum."

"For Gawd's sake get that fur coat off! You'll be roasted. Yes, I'd love to have known that Dr. Gardner. Sounds a lovely man."

Lovely? Dirty old sod, I should have thought! Getting a cheap thrill out of initiating pretty young girls into his covens and putting them through his rituals bollock-naked. Sorry, vulva-naked, I should say. Although, come to think of it, that's quite a toothsome prospect.

"I see you've got one of his books on your shelf," I remarked.

"That's right. Now you just have a look and tell me which one's you'd like." While I looked Jenny struggled out of her precious coat and the two women began discussing what seemed to me ultra-mundane and totally unexciting subjects for witches, for I assumed that they *were* witches. They were chewing the fat about what to have for Sunday lunch, the price of children's shoes, and suchlike. After a minute or two I'd selected Rollo Ahmed's *The Black Art,* Francis King's *Ritual Magic in England,* Maurice Bessy's *Pictorial History of Magic and the Supernatural,* H.T.F. Rhodes's *The Satanic Mass,* and Harry B. Wright's *Witness to Witchcraft.*

"You've missed two of the best," commented Mrs. Upton. "'Ere, take these." She picked up Arthur Waite's *Book of Ceremonial Magic* and *The Secret Lore of Magic* by Sayed Idries Shah and handed them over to me. I made suitable thank-you noises and clutched them to my bosom.

How I got myself into such a position I couldn't quite say. That is, I don't remember the actual step-by-step progress. No sooner had Jenny left us to fetch Wayne in off the street and put him to bed than I seemed to find myself lying on the settee with my head in Mrs. Upton's lap. I was reminded of the housewife who wrote to some woman's agony column saying 'before I knew where I was I found myself on the lounge floor having intercourse with the man next door.' Well, I wasn't exactly having intercourse , but I was having my forehead stroked and the muscles on either side of my neck gently massaged.

"Mrs Upton, I –"

"Aggie, please. Don't want to stand on ceremony, do we?"

"No. Well, Aggie, I – "

"What? What is it, George? Mmmm?" I felt as if I'd suddenly landed in the middle of a TV comedy.

"It's just that I don't think we. That is, that I should, er – "

Relax George. Just relax," she murmured, as she continued the soothing treatment. The feeling of TV comedy deepened. "Your neck is terribly tense, you know. There, let me loosen your tie."

I protested, albeit feebly. Actually, I was in two minds. Like any man I wouldn't turn up my nose at the idea of a woman taking my head in her lap, loosening my tie, and any further attentions that I might fantasize. But at the same time I found Aggie somewhat off-putting. There was her coarseness, the stale-cigarette-smelling breath, the strong animal scent of her, and the wrinkles and sagging cheeks which no amount of warpaint could hide. Then when I closed my eyes and breathed through my mouth, I was aware only of the heat of her thighs and the softness of her uncorsetted belly under my head. Her rise and fall against my left ear produced the inevitable rise in me, with no prospect of a fall, as far as I could tell.

She pulled off my jacket and her neck massage extended to the areas of my shoulders, upper arms and chest.

As I said, I can't account for all the intervening stages, but I came fully to my senses when Aggie began dabbing at the carpet, the settee, my trousers, and me, in that order, with the proverbial feminine scrap of lace-edged handkerchief. Then she tutted and, leaving it draped over my now detumescent member like a soggy dishcloth over a kitchen tap, went out in search presumably, of more effective material. She came back with a roll of absorbent paper and silently handed it to me.

"But why, Aggie?" I whispered. "Why not you? Why wouldn't you let me, you know, even touch you?"

"Sid. 'Cause of Sid," she replied succinctly. "Be home any second. 'Fact, that's him now." A car stopped on the drive. I heard a handbrake viciously applied.

"Oh God!" I squeaked, hastily covering my organ, still adorned with festoons of flower-patterned tissue.

"Stay in there," muttered Aggie. "He always goes straight through to

51

the back first. I'll get you out, don't you worry. Unless you want to meet him?"

"No, no, not at the moment, if you don't mind."

"You just stay put, then." She closed the lounge door behind her and I heard the front door open and click to and a man's voice saying something about 'the bleeders ain't pay ing again' and then a chink of bottles and glassses in the next room. A moment later Aggie reappeared and ushered me silently out of the house. Very cool she was, I must say. Sid couldn't have had an inkling.

"Come round tomorrow afternoon," she whispered at the door, "or any afternoon. Late-ish. But not too late!"

I nodded and scuttled off.

My relationship with Aggie was an unusual one. The normal pattern of clandestine meetings, drinks at out-of-the-way pubs, stolen afternoons in bed when hubby was safely at work, were not for us. In fact it would be inaccurate to describe us as lovers, at all. Collaborators or, better still, fellow-experimenters, is what we really were.

She was completely sold on the witchy thing. And I found that any sex with her was only to be had in the context of magic ritual. Sex was merely a by-product, as it were.

She would show me marked passages in her books, especially in her well-thumbed copy of *A Handbook of Practical Day-to-Day Witchdraft* by Joinville Stokes, and say how she'd love to try such and such a ceremony. She reminded me of the studious young bride who held her sex manual in one hand and her husband in the other. Aggie would place her book conveniently on the coffee table while we went through the prescribed actions and prayers, but she would constantly be referring to it and often she would pick it up and read aloud from it, still balancing in the correct devotional attitude.

Mind you, I was not backward myself. I'd soon read all the books she'd loaned me. And I was quicker than she to adapt ideas from them, more imaginative and, especially, at devising titillating little rituals for my own, er, titillation.

52

It occurred to me that with my particular gifts, my enthusiasm, my imagination allied to a now-extensive knowledge, and my intelligence, I was surely cut out to be roaring success in the witchcraft business.

Chapter 7

AFTER a couple of weeks or so Jenny joined us. In our excursions into ritual, I mean. I was looking forward to this as I quite fancied her. Not that she was what I'd call an attractive woman. Actually she was a bit scruffy, a bit on the grotty side, but she exuded a certain cheap sexiness that appealed to the lower side of my nature.

Yet I was doomed to disappointment. For one thing Aggie kept us both hard at it, making us keep to both the spirit and the letter of the book, and for another Jenny gave me no encouragement. I don't suppose she fancied me in the way that I fancied her. Or in any way at all, come to that. Couldn't blame her either, I told myself, looking at my reflection in the full length mirror in my bedroom. Greying greasy hair, double chin, sloping thin shoulders, paunch, thin legs, flat feet. God! What a vision of loveliness!

Nevertheless, she was a willing first initiate into the coven. Our coven. The coven of which Aggie was high-priestess, and I – resplendent in a robe made out of black-out material, with designs cut out and laboriously sewn on by myself – I, mage and scholar, was the high-priest"

Aggie's lounge, with its cheap knick-knacks, afforded hardly the right *ambience* for occult business. Aggie drew the curtains, though there was hardly a soul about in Shrewsbury Drive.

Shrewsbury, I should add, abutted on to Horton Close where I lived. Its semi-detached houses were indistinguishable from those of any new-ish development in any large village in the Midlands, or indeed of

54

such sprawling estates as Boley Park or Netherstowe in Lichfield. No picturesque timbered and thatched cottage here, as I would have wished, where we might more fittingly call upon spirits native to the fabric of the building.

The inhabitants of these houses, I guessed, were non-descript, ordinary folk, with a few harmless pretensions. What I was unable to predict, in these early days, was how such ordinary people might suddenly change their spots, how these ordinary-seeming streets might become hotbeds of vicious gossip.

As I performed the actions of the Initiation I felt the heady wine of power flow through my veins. And, naturally, as I bestowed the fivefold kiss upon the feet, knees, genitals, breast and lips of a slightly-shivering Jenny, I felt other, no less delicious, sensations. This was the stuff, I told myself! But what a pity the Initiation was a once and for all act. I felt that we were limiting ourselves by this, merely aping the rules governing the Christian sacraments of Baptism and Confirmation. If we witches liked something, should we not feel free to do it again and again? But Aggie disagreed. And I allowed her to overrule me.

At Jenny's Initiation the question of names came up. In fact there was a hold-up when we came to the part where she was to be given her witch-name because none of us had done our homework I hastily went into conference with Aggie.

"What do you think?" I whispered. "What are we going to call her?"

"The book says she should choose her own name."

"I dare say. And what did *you* choose, for yourself? And what about me? I'm supposed to be the high-priest and I haven't got a name either."

"Well choose one, quickly!" she hissed.

"Felix," I said. It was the first name I could think of. Latin origin, anyway. Meaning happy, fruitful. Quite suitable really, for the new me.

"I fancy Buttercup, for myself," said Aggie.

"Buttercup?"

"Why not? It's a flower-name. Witches have a special, what d'you

55

"All right, if you must. And Jenny?"

"I'll ask her." She went into a huddle with her daughter. "She'll take the name of Poppy," she announced. Oh my God! What a bright pair of bitches. Buttercup and Poppy!

Jenny must have seen the look on my face, though she saved her remarks until after the ceremony. "'Im and 'is Felix," she muttered to her mother. "Blooming cat food!"

Chapter 8

ONE month and several experimental ceremonies later, the question of increasing our numbers came up.

"Can't hardly call this a coven, can we? Just the three of us?" demanded Aggie.

"We need more *men*, that's what we need," said Jenny.

"All right, all right, point taken," I said. "One high-priest, one high-priestess, and one member can hardly be called a thriving coven. We must do a spot of, ah, recruiting."

"I wonder who else we could get?" said Jenny. She had a far-away look in her eyes, dreaming no doubt of men younger and more handsome than me. Not too hard to imagine, as most men <u>are</u> younger and more handsome than me!

"Well, George? How are you going to set about finding people?" asked Aggie, gathering up our ritual paraphernalia from the lounge floor. We were at Jenny's house.

I had no answer to that one, so I said the first thing that came into my head, to gain time. "Same way as I found you, my dear Buttercup."

"What? Oh, I see. You mean the way we met in the mobile library

"Naturally."

"But you can't spend all day hanging about in there to see what books people take out, looking over their shoulders at their tickets. Besides, they wouldn't start talking to you like I did."

"True, true. But I shall, I shall, (here inspiration smote me like a cricket ball between the eyes. Well? Why not?) I shall find out who reads books on The Craft in this village.."

"How are you going to do that?" Jenny looked pityingly sceptical.

"I shall go to the counter and ask," I replied.

The young lady librarian was unexpectedly forthcoming. No chance of a look down her blouse on this occasion, as she wore a high-necked sweater. But her information more than made up for this small disappointment. Did I say small? They were quite a handful, actually. MISS ANGELA ADCOCK, it said on a small counter plaque. Ah well, only to be expected.

"Oh, you'd be surprised," she said. This was in answer to my oblique reference to people reading 'that sort of book'. "You'd be surprised how many *do* read them. Yes, there's quite a lot of witches living in this village." But seeing my incredulous look, she added, "Of course, I don't know whether they really *are* witches or not. What I mean is that they borrow books on witchcraft."

Really? How interesting. I bet they're all people I know, as I know practically everybody in the village." Hint, hint. And it worked"

"Well, there's Mrs. Smirke, for a start. She lives in the same road as you. And there's her mother. They *look* like a pair of witches, I always think." So do I, and though I know that they do in fact live up to their looks I don't trouble to enlighten Miss Adcock.

"Oh my God! If they're a sample of the local witches I don't think I'll bother to join!" I replied. All good, clean jocular stuff. "Can't you do any better than that? Ha ha."

"Well, I don't know that I ought to be discussing people's choice of books behind their back."

"Oh, come. It's harmless enough."

"But we did have a man in here a few weeks ago, not a local man, who was asking about witches. Even asked me if I was a witch!"

"The idiot! Must have been some sort of crank."

"Yes. Probably asked me because I've got long hair."

"I expect so. But who else is er, interested in the subject? It's quite all right to tell me: I'm highly respectable, you know. Local schoolmaster, founder member of the Philatelic Society, and all that."

"Oh, I know you're all right, Mr. Whitehouse. Now let me see. Oooh

– you'd never believe it – there's three more people living in your road! Mrs. Meade and her husband, and Mr. Clundon. There – you wouldn't think he'd read books on witchcraft, would you?"

"No? I see what you mean, though. Pillar of the community, lay-preacher and magistrate, and so on."

"Yes. But *he* reads more than anybody. Apart from you, that is."

"Me? Ah, yes. Well, that's different. I'm thinking of writing a book on the subject. That is, a historical survey of it, you know".

"Oh, I see. So that's why you keep ordering books about it? I did wonder."

"And now you know. All academic and respectable. Ah, well, must be off. Sorry to have taken up so much of your time. Good night, Miss Adcock."

"Good night, Mr. Whitehouse."

Well I'll be damned Maurice Clundon! Wonder if he thinks his reading habits are a secret? In fact, as he's a J.P. I'd have thought it would have been wiser for him to have borrowed books on witchcraft from somewhere else. Though come to think of it, that applies equally to me. After all I belong to the group beloved of the scandal rags the juicy trinity of schoolmasters, scoutmasters and vicars.

Don't fancy Clundon much, actually. Hardly a desirable acquisition for the coven. Might've known he was the type, though. Hilary always says he's got peculiar eyes, undresses her as he looks at her, she says. Disgusting1 Unless it's me who's doing the undressing.

But Helen Meade, now she's in a different category. As a matter of fact I wouldn't mind initiating her.

59

Chapter 9

"YOU can come and have a go at mine when you've finished, Helen," I said.. I was standing looking down Helen Meade's dress as she knelt in her front garden, weeding.

I glanced up and down the road. Horton Close was deserted, but for the two of us. Good. An interruption seemed unlikely.

"Oh, it's you," she said straightening up. "You gave me quite a surprise, George." She smoothed a wisp of hair from her forehead. Fine and sandy-ish hair, not a variety I care much for. I puffed at my pipe and took stock of her. About 32, small, medium build – sound like a copper, don't I? Elfin face, quite full breasts but not very well supported, rather hippy, and pale blue eyes. Not so dusty, really. But there were two off-putting features: slightly bulging eyeballs and a deathly pale skin. It's true that I'm not exactly a sun-bronzed Adonis myself, but I do like women to be tanned a little. I refer to browning of the skin caused by exposure to sunlight, not to kinky corporal punishment. Helen's skin, where it showed to mid-thigh and halfway down her breasts, was as white as alabaster. She'd really suffer if she were to lie out on a beach in a bikini.

"Well, airck-chually.." She affected a ladylike drawl which didn't sit too well on her Brummy accent. "Airck-chually, I'm not all that keen on gardening. But I suppose Jim does so much for me." Too bloody right, he does He's a little domestic slave. The idle bitch only has to feel a bit off colour with the curse and she retires to bed for a couple of days, leaving Jim to cope with cooking, cleaning, kids, the lot!

"Ah, yes. Fair's fair," I remark, tamping down the tobacco in my bowl and fishing for my box of Swan Vestas. "Can't say I'm much of a gardener, myself. Rather read a good book any day." Here we go, craftily leading up to my real business. "By the way, read any good books lately?" Keep it light and facetious, dangle the old baited hook.

"Reading? Me? With a house, husband, and two children to look after?"

"I've got a fascinating book out of the library at the moment. It's by a chap called Gerald Gardner." Scan her face for any sign of reaction. Yes! Affected smile replaced by thoughtful look. "Yes, it's called *Witchcraft Today,*" I added. I have deliberately named what is probably the most widely-read book in the whole of Occultism, and one which I know is in and out of the mobile library like a yoyo. Though it's not as up-to-date as its title suggests. Absolutely fascinating! You ought to read it sometime."

"I have read it," she replied quietly. Yoicks! A bite! All that remains is to haul in the catch.

"Have you? Have you really? What did you think of it? Did Jim read it? Well, I'll be damned! I never dreamed I'd be lucky enough to meet anybody with the same peculiar taste in books as myself." That's the stuff. Bags of enthusiasm. Rush her off her feet.

"I don't think it's all that peculiar, reading a book on witchcraft," she replied.

"No, no, of course you don't. Nor do I. I only meant it would seem peculiar to some people. You know, the old fuddy-duddies, the stick-in-the muds, the all pi and anti-everything brigade."

"God, yes! You're so right. People like that make me sick! Live and let live, I say. If people want to read about witchcraft, so what?" she added, shrugging her slim shoulders.

"Or even participate in it," I put in quickly, "that is, practise it, *actively.* As you put it, so what? The days of persecution are over, thank God."

"Yes, thank God," she echoed, a trifle vaguely. She smoothed a wisp of hair again and looked round a little agitatedly. Had I lost her? Or had I hit the nail on the proverbial by mentioning "practising" it?

"Look here," I went on, determined not to let the conversation founder, "I've got quite a selection of books on *The Craft* – we call it

61

simply *The Craft,* you know – and you're more than welcome to borrow them. Why don't you pop over some time and I can show you?"

"Really, George! Do you want me to get a reputation?" There's nothing she'd love more dearly, I felt sure. "I'm a decent married woman, I'll have you know. I wouldn't dream of doing anything without Jim."

"Of course you wouldn't. I meant the *two* of you. Pop over this evening. Hilary will be –

"Don't tell me. Out. Well, I'll see what Jim says."

"Good, good. And I must be getting along now."

"Especially as you've just spotted your better half coming down the road?" I hadn't actually noticed Hilary, but thought I might as well play along.

"True. Don't want to get a reputation, do we? Anyway, look forward to seeing you later on."

"Don't bank on it. We might. And then we might not."

I could have banked on it, as it turned out. The Meades pottered across the road – they lived directly opposite – at about half past eight.

Hilary had gone out. Officially, if anybody came to the door being nosy, she'd gone to see her mother. In truth, she was out with Freddie, or I should say, acknowledging his recent promotion, Sergeant Freddie Osborne, stalwart of the local Specials.

Officially, too, the Meades came over, in their gardening gear, to enquire whether my shears were any better than theirs, and if they might borrow same. In fact, they were interested in my books on *The Craft.* This soon became apparent as I chatted to them through my open lounge window.

"Hear you've got some interesting books, like," remarked Jim. He had a slow, rustic way of speaking. Taught Art and Craftwork at a local secondary school.

"Yes, yes, indeed. Helen's obviously told you about our little conversation just before tea."

62

"Oh, ar. She told me as how you said you've got a lot of dirty books (he pronounced it "bewks"), books about naughty fertility rites, and suchlike."" Did she, by Gad? The little minx!"

"Have I? I don't remember saying that. Of course there are chapters on all aspects of, er, occult practices, all the various kinds of ceremonies, you know. But you must come in, both of you. We can't talk properly like this."

I took my elbows off the window sill, deposited my pipe in the giant cut-glass ashtray that I use, and went to let them in.

"Here, do sit down. Sit by me on the settee, Helen. Not to worry, Jim old man, she's quite safe with me. Ha, ha! You stay there, you've got the best chair in the house. Now, what will you have to drink? Can of lager suit you, Jim? Helen? We've a bottle of white wine open from Sunday lunch. Good. Back in a tick."

I smiled to myself as I poured drinks in the kitchen. 'Jim, old man' and 'back in a tick' my foot! Sounded like a character in some corny radio play. But all done with intent, believe me. It's a well-known fact that cliches help to make people feel at ease in an unfamiliar situation. Touch of the familiar. Reassuring, you see. One of the oldest salesman's ploys in the world. And that was what I was, no less; a salesman. I was about to sell my coven, my creation, to these poor unsuspecting simpletons.

I walked in carrying a tray balanced on the tips of my spread fingers, the tea towel with which I'd polished the glasses draped over my arm.

"Very good, Jeeves. Put it down there," said Helen.

"Used to be a waiter. When I was a student, in the long vac, you know," I said jovially.

"Cheers."

"Cheers."

The three of us drank.

"Well, I'm delighted to hear that you're both interested in my own favourite field of study," I began. Avuncular tone, easy manner. "Keep it up, George. "Yes, I've been a student of *The Craft* for a number of years now," I went on, "but I must say I've never had the good fortune to meet many people with the same interest.   Anyway, have a good browse along the shelves, and I do want you to feel free to borrow anything that takes your fancy."

"How many have you met?" broke in Helen. It was a regular habit with her, the dramatic interjection, one of her ways of getting herself noticed.

"How many? What? How many what?" I replied rather vaguely.

"Witches. Witches, you clot!" she said. Clot? Me, a clot? Can't say I liked the sound of that! Quite unsuited to my dignified status. Never mind. Time to put her in her place later.

"Dozen and a half, two dozen. Couldn't tell you the exact number. Though I've lost contact with most of them, over the years."

"You mean to say you've actually attended some of these 'ere whatcha-ma-callums?" asked Jim, balancing a pile of 'bewks' on his knee.

"Sabbats," I supplied. "Or, more usually, esbats. Why, yes. I've been connected with a couple of flourishing covens." I thought briefly of my farcical contact with Peter and Tom and with Simon Chubb's crowd. Flourishing covens, my arse! But I was out to sell, and to sell one must impress.

"Do you go to one now?" demanded Helen.

"Well, not at this precise moment," I smiled.

"Don't be daft! Nowadays, I mean. Do you belong to one nowadays? Have you been to one lately?"

"Ah, well now, let me see. Not since last Saturday, the night of the full moon, that is."

"You're not pulling our legs, by any chance?" grumbled Jim.

I'm certainly not," I replied. And in any case I'd rather pull your wife's than yours I added inwardly. "In fact – but wait a minute. Can I be sure that anything I tell you in this room would be treated as a confidence?" As if I intended to give anything away.

"'Course you can," said Jim.

"You can trust us. We can keep a secret," added Helen. Like hell! If you want anything broadcast, then tell it to a woman, in strictest confidence, especially a woman like Helen Meade.

"All right. Well, I happen to be going along to a little gathering on Friday evening. If you'd care to join me you'd both be extremely welcome.

I was doubtful about having Clundon. When I say 'having' him, naturally I don't mean in that sense, I mean as a member of the coven. I cordially disliked the fellow. There he was, out on the front, next door but one, with the bonnet of his car up. God knows what for. He wouldn't know a battery from a big end. I watched him.

Noted with amusement the anxious look which creased his normally smooth brow. Smooth, yes, smooth was the word for him. A real smoothie, was our Maurice. Oily, Hilary says. Has a peculiar way of talking, no traceable accent, rather high voice, silky, caressing. Needn't bother to caress me with it, I muttered, nor with anything else of his.

He looked up. I thought of dodging behind the curtains, but that would have been pointless as he'd seen me. Oh God, no! he's coming over! I stayed put, leaning on the sill, smoking. He walked around the bay window and grimaced at me.

"Evening Maurice," I murmured guardedly.

"Evening, old boy. Having a spot of bother with the old jalopy. Wonder if you'd mind taking a look."

"You've come to the wrong man," I said, shaking my head. "Alfie Batters is the car expert."

"Ah, Batters."

"That's right. The man with the magic touch. Serviced my car and it felt like a Rolls compared with the way it had been."

"Hmm, yes, I don't doubt it. But he, er, well, we don't exactly see eye to eye, one might say. And in any case he's out."

I glanced across and saw that Alfie's car was not on his drive. How could it be? He was out in it with my wife, Hilary!

"But if you'd just have a quick quint, there's a good fellow."

"All right. But I don't suppose I shall know what's wrong." I put

65

down my pipe, grabbed an anorak from the hall cupboard, and walked across to Clundon's drive where his old Land Rover was standing with its innards exposed. What he was doing with a blooming great vehicle like that I never could fathom. He looked like a dwarf at the wheel of it.

"What's the trouble, exactly? What's the symptons?" I asked.

"Oh, the beastly thing won't start, not easily, anyway," he drawled. That's because you leave it out on the drive in all weathers, I thought, instead of clearing some of the junk out of your garage and putting it decently to bed at nights.

"Try it," I said. He did, but it wouldn't fire until the fifth attempt.

"Plugs are the usual thing," I remarked, feeling very superior because for once I knew more than the other chap. "Got a plug spanner?" Confident that he wouldn't have.

"Er, no 'fraid not." The vague tone of the man who wouldn't recognise one if he saw it. I began to feel a little malicious pleasure.

"I've got one. Hang on a minute and I'll fish it out," I said.

I disconnected the No 1 lead and started battling to get the plug out. While I was working away, a few moments later, with wire brush and feeler gauge, Clundon got down to his real business, which was not merely a matter of hiring me as a motor mechanic.

"Much as I dislike knocking you, old boy, when you're being so helpful," he began, "I'm afraid I've a bone to pick with you." Switch to silky menacing tone, I commented to myself.

"Oh, really?" I said.

"Yes. As a matter of fact I happen to know that you've been prying into my private affairs."

"I've been doing *what*?"

"Now come off it, old boy, you know perfectly well what I mean." I replaced a plug and said nothing. "You may well say its nothing," went on Clundon. "but quizzing young lady librarians about the borrowing habits of one's neighbours is hardly the way for a decent citizen to behave."

"We're not citizens. We live in a village," I put in mildly.

66

"Don't split hairs, old boy. You're not taking one of your English lessons. Now, the point I'm making is that this sort of underhand snooping is highly discreditable to a pillar of the community like yourself. Nor is it the proper thing for our village schoolmaster to be reading books of a dubious nature. If such behaviour were to become common knowledge."

Well, of all of the barefaced blasted cheek! I wondered for a moment if my ears were deceiving me!

"Now look here, Clundon," I began (more shades of the good old Radio Four plays) "you're in no position to threaten to smear me, or whatever else you may have in mind. In fact you're in precisely the same boat. It wouldn't do for people to know that a respectable married man, and a J.P. and lay-preacher to boot, was flirting with the black arts."

"Black arts, my foot. Are you threatening me, Whitehouse?"

"Of course not. I'm just making it clear that it's no use either of us rocking the boat. Oh, and by the way, how did you find out that I borrowed books on witchcraft from the mobile library, or that I ever knew that you did the same?"

"Ah, that. Well, I happened to mention to the young lady librarian that is, I passed a remark to the effect that I thought there could not be a very great demand for the kind of books I'd just ordered. It was then that she told me y ou had been enquiring as to who read books on, er, witchcraft," I nodded and smiled sardonically. Obviously up to the same game. Wanted to make contacts. All right, contacts he shall have.

"And having pumped the girl – no, no, don't get on your high horse – having pumped her, just as I did myself, I admit it, you learned that there was at least half a dozen of us, all living in close proximity at this end of the village, who are, shall we say, interested. I wonder how long it would have taken you to make contact with us if you hadn't had this car trouble?"

"Contact? With whom? What are you implying?"

"That there is an active and flourishing coven here in this quiet little

67

corner of commuter respectability. Yes, there is. Just that. Five of us so far. Three women, two men. So you might as well join us, as you certainly are interested, and make the numbers equal."

"I – I shall have to think about it."

"Do."

"And who are they, anyway. Your, er, witches?" I told him. His face registered distaste at Aggie Upton, but at the mention of Helen and, especially, of Jenny Smirke, I was sure I detected a lascivious look light up his dark, almost black eyes.

"You should join us," I said. "Our next esbat is this coming Saturday. You'll see me set off at about eight-thirty. Be ready to jump into your car and just follow me.

Chapter 10

WHAT a pity. It would have been so much more fitting to have found an atmospheric spot in the vastness of Cannock Chase itself. I did in fact take some trouble searching for one.

The place where Simon Chubb and the faery people met, on the east flank of Sherbrook Valley, was quite suitable in itself, but its location was too far away from the village and not easily accessible by car.

Seeking an alternative, I had started out from Milford Common and walked south-east from the car park, but the hills beyond were too bare. From the Punch Bowl, a picturesque hollow for parking beside the A513, I found woods aplenty, on Harts Hill, in Brocton Coppice, and around the north Stepping Stones. I even searched for the legendary Dick Slee's cave, though without success. Nowhere was there a secluded dell of the kind I was looking for. Although nearer than Sherbrook, the area was still not handy enough and necessitated crossing the Staffordshire and Worcester Canal, the River Sow and a railway line.

It was only by chance that my eyes strayed further north, scanning my Ordnance Survey map, until they lighted upon a handful of small woodlands, separated by fields. One or two of these were even quite close to the village. Perhaps one might even be suitable? I was lucky. The second wood that I actually visited, proved to be *the one*, Abbot's Wood, it said on the map.

Aggie and Jenny agreed, as soon as I took them there. This was to be the venue for our rites. The three of us consecrated the spot with a brief but meaningful ceremony.

I managed a brief conflab with Aggie on the next Friday afternoon, before Sid came home, and we decided upon a token initiation ceremony for our three newcomers. We would go through part of the basic ceremony but no oaths were to be sworn, no witch-names given, and none of the working tools would be presented. The latter were out anyway, as it'd be quite impossible, even if they were all dying to embrace the coven, to rustle up three sets of athames, wands, scourges and censers at such short notice.

Eight thirty-five, Saturday evening. I backed into the road and pulled away, glancing out of the corner of my eye at Clundon's house. No sign of him hovering at the windows. So, he wasn't going to follow me, I thought.

But I was wrong, because his car roared into life as I passed. The blighter had been sitting at the wheel, waiting.

At the end of Horton Close, I took the sharp bend and slowed to let him catch up. I wanted him to see which way I went at the junction with the main road. I turned. Yes, he was following. All the way to Abbot's Wood, he stuck to me like glue.

The parking space was a patch of waste ground just off the road. Its earth was packed hard by the cars of courting couples. There was a tumbledown gate at the rear opening on to an overgrown track. Aggie, Jenny and I had once tried to drive down it but found it too hazardous, especially in the matter of turning round in the dark when we wanted to come back.

Two cars were there already, Aggie's and Jim's. I had described the spot to Meades, and they knew of it all right. Probably went there in their courting days.

I got out, greeted them and waited for Clundon. He took a long time positioning the Land Rover to his satisfaction.

"Come on, it's this way," I said, opening the gate just enough to squeeze through. I closed it behind us and set off leading my little party up the rising track. The pines mde it so dark that we could barely see where we were treading. Clundon suddenly flashed a pocket torch ahead of us, one of those small things on a key ring.

"Put it out," I said.

70

"Why?

"We don't want anybody to see us going up here.

"I shouldn't think there's anybody around but ourselves," he grumbled.

"We can't be sure. Anyway, I know this path well. Just follow me." We curved around to the right and dropped steeply for a moment. By the trickle of water I knew we'd reached the bottom of the drip.

"Now we'll use our torches," I said. I produced mine and led the way off the track and alongside the stream before starting uphill again.

We reached the scheduled site and found that Aggie and Jenny had already made some preparations. They'd spread out cords to mark a circle on the ground and laid a fire in the centre, twigs and branches on top of paraffin-soaked rags. Aggie did not seem to recognise Clundon, but greeted him enthusiastically, kissing him on both cheeks and taking him on one side to explain what we were going to do. Perhaps she would have done the same with Jim, but Helen stood in front of him barring the way. Or perhaps she knew the Meades already and didn't like them? I took on the job of instructing them myself, with some small assistance from Jenny.

"Maurice knows what to do now," Aggie remarked, returning to the circle.

"Good. Then I shall begin the consecration in a moment," I announced. "The three newcomers will have to stay outside the circle until called. Only we three initiates may be allowed inside. Now, Helen, you go with the ladies. Jim and Maurice come with me.

"*Must* we take all our clothes off?" demanded Helen. "*I* think it's quite chilly."

Aggie ushered her away, explaining as they went the need to cast off our clothes and with them our everyday personalities, the need to leave the body unhampered so as to be fully receptive to occult influences and vibrations.

The ceremony was a success, and I would think that this was due in no small measure to the setting in which it was enacted. Whatever discomforts we endured in terms of chill, damp and wear and tear on

71

the soles of the feet were more than offset by the stimulus we received. The clandestine feeling in the remote woodland, the feeling of being close to nature, and the harsh smell of earth and vegetation worked powerfully on our senses. As did liberal draughts of Jim's homebrew. By a punning coincidence, it was mead. I knew we should have been much more inhibited in the prosaic setting of somebody's lounge. For my own part, I always feel quite put out of the witching mood by the presence of such objects as the television, framed photos of Auntie Flo, and plaster ducks flying up the chimney piece.

Helen's complaints were silenced by the issue of navy-blue blankets which we wore as robes. All except myself, of course. I wore my black robe embroidered with cabbalistic signs.

The women returned to the edge of the circle already clad in their blankets. Aggie handed two more of them to me to pass on to Clunden and Jim. I caught only a glimpse of Helen Meade's body, a flash of white as she fidgeted with her robe, but knew that a more detailed scrutiny was on the agenda.

I cut a larger circle with my athame, moving the cord 'circle' to fit it as I went along, and carving out a hole at each of the cardinal points. I explained to our novices the name and purpose of my knife, that it was the chief working tool of the witches, and that it was usually associated with Gardnerian covens though it was referred to in the Key of Solomon grimoire. I spoke at some length of the idea of the circle standing 'between the worlds', and why it should not be entered lightly. I told them of our plans to go through a simplified, non-valid, version of the Initiation Ceremony. Then I lit the fire.

Aggie, as high-priestess, attended to Clundon and Jim. She ordered them to remove their robes and gave them a token ritual bathing by splashing them with water from a plastic beaker. Bathos reared its ugly head once more! And I did the same with Helen Meade.

The flames flickered on her whiter-than-white body. Her breasts were fuller than I'd expected, probably in contrast to her slender, rather frail limbs, and I was most intrigued by the way her nipples popped out like miniature corks at the shock of the cold water. I sluiced it across her neck and shoulders, and accidentally-on-purpose brushed one of her 'corks' with my fingertips.

The neophytes resumed their robes and watched as Aggie, Jenny and I danced, widdershins, of course, around the inside of the circle chanting the 'Eko, Eko, Azarak.'

Standing astride a small flat stone which, I explained, was the votive altar, I threw off my robe and stretched my arms upwards and outwards.

"I am Felix," I cried. And then, feeling a little foolish, I went on in a quieter voice, "Behold, as High Priest of this coven, I welcome you, you who would witness our rites and might desire soon to participate in them." I scanned the three faces, as well as I could in the dim light, for any sneers. But there were none. Probably they were conscious of Aggie and me weighing them up.

Next I rattled off a screed of gibberish in 'runic' from my Book of Shadows, whilst Buttercup raised her sword above her head.

"Bind them!" I cried dramatically, and Poppy wound cords around the wrists and ankles of the three outside the circle.

I put the ritual questions to Helen Meade and told her what her replies should be. As I was blindfolding her before leading her into the circle I managed surreptitiously to press against her, but didn't go too far with everybody watching. It occurred to me that I might be able to suggest a little private rehearsal, exclusively for the two of us, just prior to her being actually received into the coven.

I untied here ankles and led her to the four watchtowers in turn, and then back to her place where I allowed her to don her robe again.

Then Aggie performed the same part of the rite for the two men. I noticed she made a meal of tying them up and leaned heavily on each of them as she led him around the circle. I was not sure, but I thought I detected signs of excitation on Clundon's part before he covered himself.

Then followed the symbolic 'sexual and purifying ordeal'. The most, ahem, interesting section, I always feel. I drew Helen back into the circle, still bound and blindfolded, and removed her covering. As I kissed her feet I felt her shivering. At her knees I felt her tremble. When I sought her genital area she writhed a little and my mouth encountered only a tight little mat of ginger curls. O bitter disappointment! On to her breasts. I gently enclosed each of her 'corks' in turn, pinching them briefly with my encircling lips. At her mouth I felt a sharpness and remembered that she had a slight suggestion of buck teeth.

Then it was Clundon's turn. Aggie stripped him, and though he tried to hide it, it was obvious to everybody that he had an erection. Doubtless this came of watching Helen getting her kiss-blessing. Aggie then stationed Jim Meade beside Clundon. This had not occurred to me, that she might do them both together. But I could see that it would appeal to her.

I watched the three of them, fascinated. Oddly enough, this was more titillating than anything we'd done so far. Jim, I noticed, did not appear to be excited. Perhaps because the sight of me ministering to his wife was a source of jealous anger rather than of stimulation? Aggie began her work.

First she kissed each of them on their feet, and then on their knees, crouching before tham and moving from man to man easily and lightly. At each point, she 'did' Clundon first. Before his already aroused member, she paused. And to my surprise, in a loud clear voice, she intoned what I imagined to be an inspired piece of impromptu prayer.

"O Earth Mother," she cried, "Mother of us all, upon this thy son I bestow a blessing. And to his instrument of fertility, I show especial worship and devotion." Though if the truth were known I suppose she'd concocted and polished this little speech well in advance, as soon as she'd learned there were to be two new male initiates, in fact.

She brazenly caressed and kissed Clundon's organ for a full ten seconds! God! I must be honest and admit to being somewhat aroused by this performance myself. I wrapped my robe tightly about me.

Jim Meade got the same treatment. His organ progressed from semi-stiff to stiff, and then to ramrod-stiff under the high-priestess's fervent ministrations. Good God! The bitch!

74

She kissed their chests quickly and lightly, and then fastened leech-like upon their lips, pressing her body fiercely against each of theirs. Talk about a bitch on heat! I felt quite heated myself as I watched her move from one to the other. Her body, whitish-green in the firelight like a Renoir nude, was hardly of bathing beauty proportions, but she was emphatically, asssertively female. Pendulous breasts, rounded belly and all, I could have enjoyed her ecstatically at that moment. Her flesh had a kind of raw sensuality that firmer, youthful, graceful girls could never achieve. Her obscene attractiveness-cum-repulsiveness worked upon me more strongly than any clean-limbed, healthy and wholesome figure could have done.

At last she had finished, and she led the two men back to their places and put their robes on them, also resuming her own robe.

I jerked myself away from libidinous thoughts and explained to the newcomers that they would receive, at their actual Initiation, the seven tools of The Craft, a black-handled knife (athame), a white-handled knife, a wand (to control spirits), a pentacle, a censer, a scourge (sign of power, dominance, purification and enlightenment) and a set of cords. I then ordered the traditional cakes and wine to be served, with which we were to round off our ceremony.

Buttercup seated herself between her two proteges and openly fondled them whilst they ate and drank. I attempted to fondle Jenny and Helen, but though the former responded, the latter froze me. I could feel her bristling with anger at Aggie's behaviour.

On account of this I brought the proceedings to a hastier close than I had intended, fixed a date when we might meet again, and ascertained whether or not the three novices wished to become full members. They did, although in Helen Meade's case there was a certain reluctance and resentment.

We removed all traces of our Rite, even replacing the sod which had been lifted when the fire was made, and trudged back to the cars. The night rang with the slamming of doors and choruses of 'Blessed Be', the witches' hail and farewell.

Chapter 11

I SHALL not bother to give any detailed account of our next two meetings. Suffice it to say that a good rime was had by the high priest and, I believe, by the others, too. But the meeting after that provided us with a rather unpleasant shock.

We were gathered together in the same spot, in Abbot's Wood. The chief business of the night was an Invocation of Spirits. Jim, Helen and Maurice Clundon, now fully initiated into the coven, stood inside the circle with the rest of us.

Especially for the occasion I'd mugged up a number of prayers and ornate speeches from Sayed Idries Shah. Though of course I no more expected any spirit to materialise than I expected to be able to fly over the treetops on my way home. Nor did I expect any any of our requests to be heard, let alone be granted. Because, let's face it, there's nothing there, or anywhere *to* hear them. Personally I'm an agnostic, and as for Any stirring of the hairs at the nape of the neck, icy tremors, palpitating heartbeats that I've experienced at odd moments – such as when watching scary films, exploring old buildings, or walking down dark and lonely roads – these I can only attribute to some last remnants of superstition which my education has been unable to expunge. Sheer balderdash, the lot of it.

But I digrress. As I mentioned, I'd mugged up some suitable prayers. I'd had special signs embroidered on my robe, by Aggie, who used a 'consecrated needle', naturally. Signs like this:-

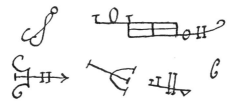

In lieu of the specified magician's white slippers, I'd blancoed my old tennis pumps and drawn the following signs on them with a red felt-tip:-

On my crown, made out of white card purloined from the school stockroom, I'd printed YRVH at the front, ADONAI at the back, and EL and ELOHIM on the right and left, respectively.

Though I begrudged the time spent, and once had to scuttle my handiwork hastily away when Hilary came home earlier than I expected, I made crowns for my disciples, decorated with the prescribed signs:-

Whilst my disciples watched, I inscribed the Triangle of Solomon on the ground, into which the spirits were to be conjured. Inside the triangle and tangential to it I drew a circle in which we witches were to stand whilst we negotiated with the spirits. Both of these marks, virtually invisible, we covered with cords. As any writing would not show up on the ground either, I laid down prepared strips of card bearing the names PRIMEMATON, ANEXHETON and TETRA-GRAMMATON along the outsides of the triangle, and smaller strips with EL, MI and CH inside the corners.

Each member of the coven held a card pentacle with a design appropriate to their spirit. I had drawn all these myself, from the *Lemegeton* of Solomon, the Book of Spirits. I myself had a pentacle pinned to my robe, by means of which, according to Shah, love can be caused in a person of one's choice merely by displaying this pentacle, which contains a Latin quotation from Genesis. It looked this this:-

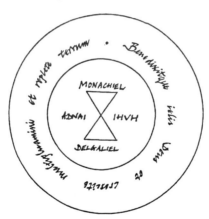

Under my guidance each of my followers had selected spirits whose powers coincided with their own personal wishes. For instance, Aggie was to invoke Amon, a powerful marquis (the Solomonic hierarchy was based upon earthly titles) who would appear as a wolf with a serpent's head or tail, and whose functions were the reconciliation of enemies, the causing of love and the telling of the future. Helen favoured Asmoday, a king with three heads – ram, bull and human – who is said to answer any question put to him. Though what profound poser *she* was likely to put I couldn't think.

Maurice Clundon, though I told him of potential dangers, insisted upon Belial, who could help him towards wordly promotion and make him receive favours. This spirit, I warned him, also has the alarming fault of desiring all, including the operator himself, and moreover expects sacrifices. Jim Meade bore a device of Halpus, an earl, who punishes sinners with the sword. I was surprised at him, at Jim, not Halpus. Would this be a streak of the fire and brimstone mentality handed down from his Calvinistic ancestors? Jenny chose Sitry, a prince who can 'cause man to love woman and vice versa'. Finally I myself plumped for Zepar, a strong duke, hoping he would fulfil his promises of 'changing people into any shape they desire', perehaps of transforming me from a paunchy, balding, middle-aged slob into a handsome Mr.Universe and 'making a woman love any man, at his command' perhaps serving Helen Meade's body up to me on a plate. Odd how I now found her desirable again, in view of the frustrating nature of our little affair months ago. Must be because of my new status as high-priest gave me a feeling of power over her, a feeling that she was mine to command instead of to be pleaded with on bended knee and crooked elbow.

We took up our positions and the Invocation began.

Taking off my robe and swirling it around in the air before settling it again upon my shoulders, I opened our conjurations in a clear, strong voice.:

"Through the symbolism of this garment I take on the protection

THEODONIAS, ANITOR, O ADONAI, cause that my desire shall be accomplished, by virtue of thy power. To thee in praise and honour for ever and ever. Amen."

Here I paused and each one of us concentrated upon his or her own personal objective, muttering under our breath the name of our appropriate spirit. Each of us held a wand, to 'control the spirit', as the book has it. We stood facing the corners of the triangle, a pair of us to each corner. What a hell of a shambles it'll be, I thought, if all six of our spirits were to materialise simultaneously! Though I certainly didn't think there was a snowball in hell's chance of even one of them appearing.

Helen Meade and I stood close together. Had to, there wasn't much room. And as I muttered 'Zepar' I could both feel and see her dithering beneath her robe. Everybody had graduated from blankets to curtain material by now, but though they looked more elegant they were undoubtedly chillier. Whilst I muttered 'Zepar' I must admit that my eyes were not upon the space where he might appear, but upon Helen, as were my thoughts.

With an effort I dragged my mind back to the business in hand, and launched into the rigmarole known as the Exhortation of the Spirit.

"O Spirits ANOOR, AMIDES, THEODONIAS, ANITOR O ADONAI, I conjure thee, empowered with the strength of the Greatest Power, and I order thee by BARALAMENSIS, by PAUMACHIE, APOLORESEDES, and by the most powerful Princes Genio, Liachide: the Ministers of the Tartar Seat, commanding Princes of the Throne of Apologia, in the ninth place!"

"I conjure thee, O Spirits ANOOR, AMIDES, THEODONIAS, ANITOR, O ADONAI, by He whose Word created, by the Strong and Highest Names of ADONAI, EL, ELOHIM, ELOHE, SABAOTH, ELION, ESCHERCE, JAH, TETRAGRAMMATON, SHADDAI – appear immediately here so I may see thee, in front of this circle, in pleasant and human forms, without any unpleasantness!"

"Come at once, from any part of the World; come pleasantly, come now, come and answer thou our questions, for thou art called in the Name of the Everlasting, Living and Real God, HELIOREM."

"Likewise I conjure thee by the name under which thou knowest thy God, and by the name of the Prince and King who rules over thee"

"I conjure thee to come at once and to fulfil our desires, by the proverbial Name of Him who is obeyed by all, by the Name TETRAGRAMMATON, JEHOVAH, the names which overcome everything, whether of this world or any other: come, speak to us clearly, without duplicity; come, in the Name of ADONAI SABAOTH: come, linger not. ADONAI SHADDAI, the King of all Kings, commands thee!"

At this point Helen Meade's robe, which she'd been trying to adjust, slipped from her shoulders and fell to the ground revealing her in all her alabaster nakedness. Naturally my eyes shot out like the proverbial chapel hatpegs, to focus upon her 'corks' and her tiny triangle of curls. Thus it was that I didn't see what Helen saw until she frantically clawed at my arm.

"God! How awful!" she cried, gouging her nails into me. I looked up and saw....Christ! My heart jumped into my mouth. There on the edge of the light was a figure. It seemed immensley tall. The head was in shadow. But the trunk... My God! White ribs. A skeleton! Death himself had come for us!

Then the thing spoke.

"Well I'll be buggered! So this is what you lot have been getting up to". It stepped into the space allotted to Separ and Asmoday. Harvey. Ronald Harvey! Wearing a black Fair Isle sweater with white hoops around it and a dark tie hanging down in front like Yogi Bear. So much for his 'ribs'.

Chapter 12

AND then there were seven. Rather like the ten little nigger boys, sorry, black boys, but in reverse.

Ron Harvey was normally a quiet sort of chap, quieter than you'd expect from the look of him. His height, over six foot, his broad shoulders and deep chest, and his rather handsome well-shaped head, complete with heavy black library frames and magnificent sideburns, indicated a deep and forceful voice. In actual fact his voice was a bit higher than average and he spoke unnaturally quietly. I remember reading somewhere that really violent characters were often deceptively quiet on the surface. Of course I had no evidence that Harvey was in fact a violent man. I'd heard nothing about him ever attacking anybody. But he looked as if he could. He had huge meaty hands and I once saw him push his car into the garage as easily as pushing a pram It was his manner, though, that worried me: the unnatural soft-spokenness of him, the feeling that he could explode without warning. I didn't know it then but I was due for more than one moment of anxiety on this account.

On the night when he burst in upon us he was actually enjoying himself. For once he was loud. And I could tell from the moment he opened his mouth that he'd been on the beer. He told us, guffawing, that he'd been wondering about the comings and goings for some time, and that he'd decided to satisfy his curiosity by following us.

"Jesus! The witches of Horton Drive, eh?" he said. "Who'd believe it? A respectable, law-abiding shower like you lot! Anybody'd think

82

butter wouldn't melt in y'mouths. And here you are all prancing around bollock naked. Ker-rist! There's plenty of people who'd get a shock if they got to hear about these goings on."

He 'had us by the short and curlies', as he himself put it. What were we going to do about it?

"Now look here – " began Clundon, pompously.

"Hold it a moment, Maurice," I broke in, "you're not on the bench now –"

"Not on the bench'!" shouted Harvey. "I like that. Not on the flaming bench! Well, he wouldn't be, would he? All starkers like that. They'd run him in. Then he'd look a silly little J.P., not half! Ha, ha!"

"I don't see why I should tolerate –" began Clundon again.

"Can't do a bloody thing about it," retorted Harvey. "What can you do, eh? What're you going to do?"

"There's only one thing we can do," I said quietly. This steadied Harvey.

"Yeah?" he said.

"Yes. Offer you a drink. Get the sherry out, Aggie."

The upshot was that he joined us. I knew how to get round him.

I insisted that he came to our next meeting. I whispered to Jenny and Aggie to give him a bit of attention, which they did. After I'd plied him with practically a whole bottle of sherry he was friend and ally for life. How he drove his car home, God knows. But he managed it, without mishap.

At our next meeting he was fully initiated. He took the name of 'Fortis', at my suggestion.

Chapter 13

"ARE you going to Annette's party?" asked Helen brightly. We were chatting on her drive, ostensibly about gardening, actually about our next esbat, with appropriate 'ooh's and 'aah's at our reminiscences of Ronald Harvey's jack-in-the-box appearance at the last one.

"Who?" I replied.

"You know, Annette Hamlyn, Shrewsbury Avenue, husband left her, she's got a boy and a girl, both went to your school. You know, she used to be a model."

Yes, I knew. One of the village *femmes fatales*. Everybody, that is, all the women, had something derogatory to say about her. Therefore I was in favour of her, on principle.

"Not as far as I know," I said.

"Not as far as you know? Oh, going to the party, you mean. But you must, you simply *must* go! I know, I'll ask her to invite you. I shall be having coffee with her tomorrow morning. I'll ask her then."

"You needn't bother, really," I said. "I'm not exactly the party type."

"Oh, but you are! You are! You enjoyed yourself at *my* party."

I suppose I did. It was the first time I'd actually been unfaithful to Hilary. Not that I hadn't already committed countless adulteries in my mind with the most unlikely of females. Hilary had already had two lovers, herself. But although I knew this, and she knew I knew, I'd made no move for a long while. And perhaps wouldn't have done so to this day, but for Helen Meade's friend Julia, who'd thrown herself at me. I won't dwell upon such sordid details as smoochy dancing with the lights down low, at the party, and a couple of brief visits to an empty bedroom for a more prolonged embrace. Anyway she wouldn't

84

come across, neither then nor on the one frustrating occasion when I took her out.

But these cavortings were sufficient, it seemed, to give Helen the idea that I liked parties.

"You'll enjoy Annette's party," she added. "Hers are always super. Better than mine, damn her eyes! You're bound to click with somebody at Annette's."

"I'm not sure that I want to click with anybody," I said, yawning.

"Nonsense! It's all you men ever think about. Anyhow, I must be going. I'll see that you get an invitation."

"It's addressed to you," said Hilary, handing me a small white envelope. " 'By hand'. A billet-doux from some woman, by the look of it."

"I doubt it," I said, reaching out for the envelope.

"So do I!" she rejoined spitefully. I took out the notelet and read it.

'Dear George,

I am giving a small party for a few friends, on Saturday evening, and wondered if you would care to come? By all means bring Hilary with you, but if you prefer to come alone, I shall understand. Either way, you will be welcome.

Yours,

Annette (Hamlyn)
54 Shrewsbury Drive'

"I've been invited to a party," I said.
"Marvellous. Whose?"
"Annette Hamlyn's."
"God! She must be getting hard up for a man, if she has to ask the

85

likes of you." The bitch! That was both vicious and uncalled for, and I was stung by it. Strange, that Hilary could still hurt my feelings at times, for she didn't mean a damn thing to me really.

"She says you can go too, if you want to," I mumbled.

"Hmm! She knows what she can do with her precious party! But I wouldn't dream of trying to stop *you*, George. *You* go, and have yourself a little orgy, like you did at the Meades'."

That was a total waste of time," I muttered.

"Quite. As you say, rubbish, the whole lot of them. But you go to this little rave-up, George. You never know, you might even make it with the Hamlyn woman herself."

I went. But with no intention of 'making it with the Hamlyn woman'. As I bathed and shaved and put on a clean shirt I felt unreasonably nervous. Stupid. There'll only be the usual old faces from Horton and Shrewsbury and a few odds and sods from other parts of the village. I suppose it must have been a tiny bit of residual shyness left over from childhood, from the days when my mother used to force me to go to parties. I remember the misery of getting ready on those occasions, the painful sensation of walking into a room and feeling that the eyes of all, especially the girls, were upon me, weighing me up for the puny and insignificant wretch that I was. And most of all, the absolute certainty that all my flies must be undone. I can actually recall standing behind sofas and armchairs in an attempt to hide my imagined shame, and running a surreptitious finger up the line of my zip to make sure it was fastened.

Some foolish remnant of this feeling stayed with me as I knotted my tie. On Annette's doorstep, ringing the bell, I involuntarily checked my zip.

Annette let me in. And there they all were. The old familiar faces. The pasty, sly faces of the would-be lechers, the smug dumpling faces of their 'tidy wives', the mean faces of the money-grubbers, and the sharp features of the gossips, the high colour of the hearties, and the

86

brittle, birdlike looks of their painted, acquisitive partners. Sounds as though I don't like my neighbours much. But this isn't the case. I only dislike some of them. Quite a few are decent, friendly, tolerant souls. Or are they? How much would they tolerate, I wonder?

I had a sudden vision of myself appearing in their midst in my full ceremonial witch's robes, with my coven lined up behind me. The picture I conjured up was so vivid that for a moment the actual scene before my eyes was eclipsed by the imagined one. But my visualising faculty must have been weak, because my disciples faded, leaving just me. That is, I couldn't picture them any longer, only myself, standing there watching the faces in front of me c rumble and change. Change into expressions of, what? Incredulity, to be sure. Then what? Distaste, hatred, anger? I'd no time to decide what their reactions were, as I was jerked back to the present, to the real situation, by somebody speaking to me.

It was a woman I knew only slightly. Penny Jones. A ginger-haired, double-chinned creature of about 35 whose black sweater and ski pants did nothing whatsoever for her lumpy figure. As soon as she caught my attention she started flapping her rubbery lips.

"Oh, George," she cried, "will you do something for me?" Holy cow! As if I would! I should think any man who'd do anything for *her* ought to see his optician, or his analyst, double-quick! But it was unlikely that she meant that sort of 'doing'.

"Do something?" I murmured, injecting the Nth degree of vagueness into my voice.

"Yes, it's pretty desperate. My Oliver's going to be in your class next year, and he hasn't learnt a *thing* since he's been with Miss Collingham. For heaven's sake, George, teach him something!"

Christ! Here's a good start to a swinging party, I thought. I muttered something about always teaching something to every child in my charge, put in a quick plug for his present teacher, pooh-poohed the idea of him learning nothing, and made my getaway as fast as possible. Revolting old bag!

I looked around for somebody reasonably pleasant to talk to.

Gwyn Evans was there, with his big booming rugger-player's laugh fooling with the women when he thought his wife wasn't looking. Helen Meade was giggling with a couple of friends and looking as if she'd had more than a few drinks already. A fellow called Drake was showing off his plastered arm and leg from a road accident and telling everybody how by his skill and presence of mind he'd saved four lives. . His wife Meryl, an attractive grey-haired nursing sister, was earnestly airing the latest theatre criticisms she'd gleaned from the *Observer*. A fat little woman called Pam Butcher was flaunting her meaty charms as she jigged to the pop music blaring out from Annette's stereo. Her long, lean husband Ray, Helen's latest passion, was dancing absently with his head just missing the chandelier. Any number of dull worthies were propping up doorways and puffing out clouds of smoke or grinding fag-ends into the carpet.

My stocktaking was pulled up short when I realised that somebody was watching *me*. Just by the lounge door two couples were in conversation, but one of the men was clearly not much involved. He looked at me very directly, before turning away with a faint smile on his face. The cheeky sod! I'm the observer, I don't want people observing *me*! Who was he?

"Who's that? Tall chap with the glasses," I asked Annette as she offered me a drink from a tray.

"Where? Oh, him. That's Edmund, a neighbour of mine."

"Edmund who? Should I know him?"

"Wheate. Edmund Wheate. Something to do with your line of business. He's a psychologist, somebody told me.."

"Aaah. Oh, thanks, I'll have a spot of dry sherry." She went on her way. So, that was Edmund Wheate. A 'dishy' man, so Hilary had described him. Helen had said the same thing. In fact she's said we ought to recruit him into the coven, now I come to think of it.

I had another good look at him. Not that I'd think of actually inviting him. But yes, he could be the type. Most people you could see, at first glance, would not more join a coven than jump over the moon. So mundane, so unimaginative and dull; such humdrummers, content with

88

their cosy little round of work, food, telly and bed. Edmund Wheate didn't belong to this category at all.

"George, you're not dancing," cried Helen, swinging on my arm. The way she spoke it sounded like 'danshing'. My guess about her hitting the bottle had been correct.

Though I was not prepared for what she said next. "Come on, George, let you hair down," she squealed. "I know you can dansh. You're like a , like a dervish when you're danshing round the bonfire in the – "

Good God! I gave here a sudden jerk that stopped her from saying 'nude', just in time!

"Be careful!" I hissed. Looking round quickly I was surprised to find that nobody had taken the slightest notice. Thank God for that.

But I could foresee trouble. The best thing to do was to get h old of Jim. I discovered him sitting at the end of a settee squashed up against the arm by a large young lady who was quite oblivious to his plight, owing to her preoccupation with her boy-friend's wandering hand.

"Here, Jim. Word in your ear," I muttered, beckoning. He prized himself out of his seat and followed me. There didn't seem to be anybody in the kitchen so I led him in there.

"It's Helen. She's, you know, a bit sloshed, isn't she?"

"No idea. Haven't seen her for ages." Well I had. She'd been slopping all over her lanky lover Ray, in the lounge with the lights down lecherously low. Annette had put on a smoochy L.P. for the benefit of couples y oung enough to still want to neck, and for those who had the nerve to neck publicly with other people's spouses.

"Take it from me, she is," I said gravely. "And her tongue's loosened, to put it mildly. She's probably on the point of spilling the beans to all and sundry about you-know-what. I suggest you take her home."

"Hmm. Well, I'll try," said Jim gloomily. "But she'll take a bit of persuading."

"Well, persuade her! And don't spare the heavy-handed bit, if necessary." It was on the tip of my tongue to add that wives should learn to do as their husbands told them. Though *I* would be a fine one

89

to talk, as this was hardly the case with Hilary and me.

At that moment the lady herself appeared. She nearly fell down the stairs, in fact, saving herself only by swinging crazily around the post at the foot of the banister. Jim plunged forward determinedly.

"Look, Helen. Don't you think we ought to go home?" he began.

"Don't wanna go home."

"I think I'd better take you home. You sound as if you've had too much."

"Not had too mush! Never had too mush! Going to have another. (hic). Then I'm going to find a lovely man to, to dansh with (hic)"

Jim had no chance to remonstrate further as she lurched past us into the kitchen, grabbed a bottle of ginger wine and tripped unsteadily into the smooching room, in search of Ray presumably. Jim shambled off in her wake.

I started to move in the same direction myself, when I saw Annette coming down the stairs. She spotted me, seized my arm, bundled me into the kitchen and shut the door. Leaning her shapely backside against it, she wagged a finger at me accusingly.

"I've a bone to pick with you," she said. Sounded ominous.

"Me? Why, what am I supposed to have done?"

"It's what you *haven't* done, that I'm complaining about."

"Oh?"

"Yes. I've been having a most interesting little heart-to-heart with Helen Meade in the powder room. She's been telling me what a lovely, delightful, naughty time you've been having."

"I don't know what you mean," I said, bluffing desperately. "It's obvious that she's tight, and anything that a woman, especially a woman like her, might say when she's – "

"Nonsense! You can't kid me, George. There's seven of you. Three women and four men."

"Well?" I still hadn't a clue what her attitude was.

"Well, what I want to know is this: why haven't *I* been invited to these little orgies?"

90

Chapter 14

EIGHT o'clock, the following Saturday. I picked up Annette at her house.

It was she who'd insisted upon this, with a cheerful disregard of anything her neighbours might say. As for myself, why should *I* bother? My wife Hilary went out with various men, a matter that was no secret. One could hardly expect it to be a secret in this little hotbed of gossip. So why should it matter if anybody thought, or said, that I was taking out Annette Hamlyn? Sauce for the goose, and all that. Indeed, as Annette was one of the most desirable females for miles around I ought to feel pleased that anyone might jump to such a conclusion.

I'd heard that her husband had left her more than once. The last occasion, so the story went, was on account of her going for him with thecarving-knife! This was about a year ago, and he hadn't been back. So she was hardly deceiving him when she enjoyed the various liaisons credited to her.

As we picked up speed along Shrewsbury Drive we passed two women walking in the opposite direction. They had a good look at both of us. The one said something and the other laughed. Perhaps they were echoing Hilary, for all I know, saying God, she must be getting hard up for a man! But I didn't care. I turned left at the main road and was soon out of the village.

I always feel a sense of release when I leave that place behind me. I feel free. I rejoice in the anonymity, for one thing, because in the village practically everybody knows me. All those who have children at the school, anyway. This time, however, I had the extra and, need I say, unusual, pleasure of having an exceptionally attractive woman in the car with me.

Annette was wearing a black sweater, an extremely short black skirt, dark tights and black high boots. On top of this lot she had a shiny PVC mac of peacock blue. Both mac and boots seemed somewhat superfluous to me. It was a dullish evening but warm and there was no certainty of rain. She could only be wearing them because of their sex connotation.

She was sitting rather slouchily, her elegant knees resting against the glove compartment. They were like magnets to my eyes. I hoped she hadn't noticed.

"If you must look at my knees," she said, divining my simple, crude masculine thoughts, "you'd better pull in at a lay-by, or something. Otherwise we're likely to meet another car head-on."

Her tone was a purring drawl. Obviously she'd expected me to ogle her. It was no less than her due. She was only concerned from the road safety angle.

"Yes. Ah, yes. Quite," I bumbled. In spite of my considerable command of words I always get my tongue in a knot when talking to a beautiful woman. Though I suppose Annette was not exactly beautiful. Feminine, yes, undeniably feminine and, let's face it, unequivocally sexy.

"Well, er, you shouldn't have such, er, delightful knees," I said. She smiled at my clumsy attempt at gallantry.

"Where are we going?" she asked.

"It's a little spot out in the country. Hasn't got a name as far as I know. Miles from anywhere. We have to be private, you see." She didn't pursue it. Unlike Helen, when I took her out several months ago, badgering me about my 'plans' for the evening, wanting to know it all down to the last detail, which was a damned nuisance, as I usually hadn't any plans beyond the general notion of finding a quiet pub and a suitable spot afterwards to try and enjoy her.

"And what kind of ceremonies have you got lined up? Some sort of naughty fertility rituals, are they?"

"No, no, of course not. But you don't quite know what you might be letting yourself in for."

"Oh, I shall cope," she said airily. I made no reply to this.

My remark had been meant to imply that there were dark and mysterious forces in my control towards which she would feel a certain amount of awe. Though I ought to have known that the Annette Hamlyns of this world don't awe very easily.

"Did you know that witches work in the nude?" I asked. It didn't seem to matter. She wouldn't be shocked, or frightened off, I thought. I was correct.

"I wouldn't be ashamed of *my* body, in any company," she said.

"Naturally not. And it wouldn't bother you that four men were looking at it?"

"Looking does no harm."

"And if more than just looking were involved?" I was enjoying the turn the conversation had taken. My shyness had evaporated. I felt that I could say more or less what I liked to her, so long as I took care to flatter her. All I had to do was go on confirming her opinion that she was the cat's whiskers.

"That would depend."

"Upon?"

"Upon whether I felt like doing it, whatever it was, or not."

"Quite so. Well, I think you'll enjoy yourself."

Correct again. She did enjoy herself, hugely. She was the centre of interest, and that was the main thing.

To begin with, she made an impression by telling everybody that she had asked me to initiate her right away, fully and without any kind of dummy run. Although I hadn't definitely agreed to this there didn't seem to be much point in saying so. She appeared amongst us unclothed without the slightest self-consciousness. Yet oddly enough, I didn't find her as exciting as when she was dressed, probably due to the provocative style of her clothes.

Ronald Harvey enjoyed the sight of her, though I felt sure he still had more of a letch for Helen. He'd mentioned to me more than once that

93

he hated her guts and wanted to poke her out of spite. His terminology, not mine. Clundon was licking his lips, and Jim Meade was getting a good eyeful whenever he thought his wife wouldn't notice.

I'll not dwell upon the details of Annette's Initiation. She bore the ministrations of the high-priest with aplomb. In fact I felt more than a little annoyed that she was not more respectful and, well, submissive. For all the notice she seemed to take of me *she* might have been the adept, the mage, and I the novice. I did not find the bestowal of the five-fold kiss upon her delightful parts as thrilling as I expected. To be honest, it wasn't thrilling at all. Though I expect the other three men would have gladly changed places with me for those few moments. I stole a quick glance at the faces of the other women. Helen Meade's expression was neutral. But Jenny Smirke was curling her lip in a sneer and her mother Aggie looked thunderous. I was not to know the real significance of these facials until a later occasion.

Annette took the witch-name of Primula.

And now we were eight: Felix (myself), Fortis (Harvey), Justus (Clundon – a bit corny, him being a JP), Peritus (Jim Meade – very appropriate, him being a craftsman – my suggestion, of course), and the four ladies: Buttercup and Poppy (Aggie and her daughter – a wonder she didn't choose Daisy!), Erica (Helen Meade) and finally Primula, our latest recruit.

But the business of the evening was not yet done. I had agreed to the high-priestess conducting a ritual of her own devising, one loosely described as being homage to the Earth Mother, but whose details I was unaware of. Perhaps it was a good thing I had not known what was in store. In any case I could not have evaded my part in it.

"O Mother Earth!" began Aggie, in a loud impassioned voice. "Hear our cries, listen to our supplications, we who lie upon thy bosom and embrace thee!" Lie upon thy bosom? What the devil's she on about, I was wondering, when she flung herself face downwards upon the ground. "Everybody down, like this," she hissed. There were groans. The earth where our feet had tramped was bare and a light dew that was forming was even making it slightly muddy. I was quite worried about

94

my ceremonial robe, in fact.

"Down!" hissed Aggie, and grudgingly we obeyed.

Lying prone, with a rank earthy woody scent in our nostrils, we listened while she spouted a whole rigmarole of stuff culled from God knows where.

"Mother Earth," she cried, "regard your devoted ones. Hold us in your sacred embrace. Bless us! Strengthen us! Make fertile our loins!" (Ironic this, for I'd heard that she'd had an abortion herself, in her youth. And the fact that she did eventually have just the one child, Jenny, was hardly an example of fertility. In any case surely she wouldn't want to become fertile, at the age of 52? Nor could I think of any other amongst us who would want to produce children).

"Keep us from sickness," she went on. "Keep us youthful. (Ah – much more to the point!) Give us delight in our senses as only you know how to give.

"Hear us now, see us now, as we offer unto you a threefold adoration. First, we adore you with our hearts and minds."

In a different tone of voice she instructed us, her acolytes: "Make mental prayer to the Mother, my children. Give thanks and do not be afraid to ask her for anything you have need of."

She bowed her head, resting it on her forearms, and fell silent. My own mental prayer consisted of having a quick look to see how the others were faring, and wondering what farcical tricks she'd have us doing next.

"Rise to your feet, children. Gird up your loins. (What with, for Pete's sake?) Let us praise the Goddess with our tongues and by the holy act of dancing."

At her command we formed up into a circle and started tripping the light fandango, first *widdershins* and then deasil, whilst chanting line by line after her.

"Mother blest, we thee adore,"
"Mother blest, we thee adore,"
"Upon our heads thy blessings pour;"

95

"Upon our heads thy blessings pour;"
"Keep us from affliction sore,"
"Keep us from affliction sore,"
"Make us thine for evermore."
"Make us thine for evermore."

Not bad I suppose, if it were Aggie's own composition, but even so the sheer banality of it made me wince. This and much more we parrotted whilst whirling around faster and faster until we were puffing and blowing like a school of grampuses.

"Enough!" she cried, with an imperious wave of her arm as she leapt into the centre of the circle. We cannoned into each other as we clumsily halted, and then we stood facing inwards, breathing heavily. Not the least distressed was the high-priestess herself, but she'd now got the bit firmly between her teeth and would not stop for anything.

"O Mother of us all," she gasped, "witness now how we revere you. For as you are yourself the source of all rebirth (pant, pant), all lives of plant and bird and beast, accept our homage. Behold us when we adore you with our bodies. Behold and bless us – as we now perform the holy act of life itself!"

Gripping me by the arm, she drew me into the centre of the circle beside her. "May the ritual union of your high-priestess and priest be pleasing unto you!" What-what-what? I was getting worried. She pulled my robe from my shoulders and flung her own to the ground with a grand gesture. No, no, she can't be, I told myself. I still couldn't believe it when she dragged me down on my bundled-up robe and hurled herself on top of me! Rearing up, she addressed the other six:

"You will not find favour with the Goddess! The Goddess does not love mere onlookers. Let each one of you couple with the man or woman nearest you. Follow the example of your high-priestess and priest. Pay homage to the Mother with your bodies!"

With this, she ground her face into my neck and let her not inconsiderable weight lie full upon me.

I suppose I must have pipe-dreamed of orgies, in the early days, dreams of ritual copulation with some lithe, raven-haired, abandoned and beautiful young witch. But I had nothing like this in mind. I wondered if I were dreaming for a moment. But the feel of Buttercup's teeth gnawing my ear and her bush scouring away at my groin left me in no doubt that it was real. With a sudden roll like a ship's boat on a stormy sea, she capsized, and I found myself lying gasping on top of her like a half-drowned sailor. She writhed and jigged under me, pulling my head down when she caught me looking around at the others.

"Must look! Both of us," I panted. "Must look and see how our disciples are (gasp) honouring the Goddess. You want to know, don't you?

She agreed to this, and we sat up. We looked, and saw that Jenny and Clundon were breathlessly at it, not merely following our example but well ahead of it! The pint mugs of Jim's homebrew which we'd swigged to celebrate Annette's Initiation must have had more than a little to do with it. Though the behaviour of these two wasn't so surprising: after all, here was a rare opportunity for Clundon, the respectable pillar-of-the-community type, to indulge his secret lusts; and as for Jenny, she was a little nympho, anyway.

Annette Hamlyn had Jim's head cradled in her lap and she was stroking his fevered brow. While appearing to indulge she was cleverly keeping things cool.

Ronald Harvey and Helen Meade presented the most interesting sight. He had her pinned to the ground and his hands were running all over her. She was clawing him, but not in passion, as I thought at first. She was trying to get out from under!

Although it was obvious to me that only one of these three couples was, ahem, 'coupling', the high-priestess was quite gratified by what she saw. But in another sense she was nowhere near gratified!

"You Felix, you!" she grated in my ear. "Neglecting your priestly duty, you are! You an' me should be setting the example, not 'anging back! Show a bit of manhood!" she urged, taking my semi-stiff mem-

97

ber in her hand. Good God! The agony of it! The raking of her long scarlet talons! Being a circumcised man I've always been apprehensive about manual stimulation by women, and this time did I suffer, by God, I did! Pain outweighed the pleasure by at least ten to one. Inevitably I went flaccid.

With an impatient heave she flung me overboard, jettisoned me.

"Good. Very good. An example of true worship," she muttered, bending over the spent figures of Maurice Clundon and her daughter. "Throw yourselves into it!" she screeched at Jim and Annette who were hardly touching each other. "Keep at it!" she rasped at Ronald Harvey.

"He'll do nothing of the sort! Get him off me, the beast!" squealed Helen.

"Who're you calling a beast?" grated Harvey. "Anyroad, a beast's just what you want, you little bitch – an effing donkey with an effing great phlonk about two foot long!"

"Ouoh! You animal! Get off me!" squealed Helen.

"Here, I say – " muttered Jim.

"Take it, you little bitch, take it! Honour the effing Goddess!" panted Harvey.

I began to get alarmed. What was taking place before my very eyes, to all intents and purposes, was rape. But who was I to pull Ron Harvey off her? He'd pulverize me. And in any case she was getting what she'd always deserved, the little cockteaser.

Jim abandoned Annette and was shifting about from foot to foot, not knowing what to do. I looked at Clundon. He shrugged and looked away. What could we do, any of us? We might as well tackle a maddened gorilla. Helen Meade began to scream.

What would have happened next, I can't say. But the problem was solved in an unexpected way.

Suddenly a powerful torch was flashed in my eyes, blinding me. It blinded all of us. We must have looked like startled rabbits. Then a voice came from the darkness behind the light.

"I don't know what on earth you people think you're playing at, but

98

I'll have you know you're on Private Land!" Upper-crust accent, but quavering a bit – partly with anger, but also, I guessed, through old age.

"Private! Bollocks!" shouted Harvey struggling to get on his feet. "Get that sodding light off me, or I'll bloody-well kill you!" He lunged towards the torch which dipped and lit up the ground at his feet. I could just see that it was an old boy in tweeds with a pork pie hat who was holding it.

"Now then, you," roared Harvey, seizing him by the lapels. The old chap turned round and shouted into the darkness behind him:

"Peter! Go and telephone for the police. Hurry yourself, lad! Run!"

"Stuff the police! And stuff you, you barmy old bugger!" cried Harvey, and seized the man by the throat.

At last my numbed brain began to function again. "Stop it, Ron! Leave him!" I yelled. No effect. "You'll kill him, you great ox! Think, man – they'll put you away for life! You don't want that, do you? Let him go!"

Again, I had the curious feeling that I was an actor in a film. These scraps of corny dialogue were my lines. Only this was for real!

"Let go, you fool!" I shouted. "And let's get away while we've got the chance." Harvey let him go thank God. He stood back, panting and clenching his fists.

"You'll pay for this!" (more film dialogue) gasped old Tweedy, as he staggered away into the woods.

I looked around. Good God, they'd all gone! All except Aggie and Jenny, who were bundling the paraphernalia rapidly into the holdalls they'd brought it in. When they were dressed they stalked off without sparing me a glance. I looked at Harvey. Still muttering to himself, he picked up his things and followed them.

Left alone, I put on my shoes and kicked soil over the fire.

Chapter 15

AFTER that fiasco there was a lull in the career of the coven. For one thing I had a job to find another satisfactory meeting-place. For another there was the fact that no matter what dates I put to my witches, each of them seemed to have some prior engagement.

It was about this time that the Sunday evening get-togethers with the Batterses began. At first, it was Alfie Batters who invited Hilary and me over for a drink one evening. This was on Hilary's account and not, by any stretch of the imagination, on mine. I didn't know then that he was hoping something would develop between his wife Molly and myself.

The Batterses lived on the opposite side of the road, about six doors down. Their lounge was laid out in an attempt at style – purple curved settee, orange fleecy rug in front of the stone fireplace, chrome and glass cocktail cabinet. But the effect was marred by the plaster heads of Turks and other fearsome orientals on the walls, by the fact that the stonework around the bay window was made of plastic, and by such homely touches as 'A present from Clovelly' and a pokerwork plaque saying 'Molly and Alfie live here.'

Alfie was in casual rig, navy Terry-towelling shirt with a criss cross white cord at the neck and check trousers, slightly baggy. His hands were meticulously scrubbed clean of the grime acquired in his favourite hobby of servicing other people's cars. Molly was in a tight pink crimplene dress. She'd fairly trowelled on the make-up and ponged like a chemist's shop.

"Ah well, here we are, here we are! What are we going to have to drink? Hilary? My word you look a stunner in that dress. Cor, I couldn't half fancy you!"

100

"Behave yourself, Alfie Batters, and get the folks a drink," said Molly, preening herself.

I knew her slightly, enough to make a formal introduction unnecessary. But I'd never actually heard her at close quarters. As we exchanged pleasantries about the jolly old weather, I was quite taken with the huskiness of her voice. Made her sound rather sexy. It was only later I learned that it was caused by asthma.

Alfie insisted upon my having a pint of bitter – he'd bought in a gallon can specially for the occasion. I was reluctant, as beer invariably gave me hangovers, but took the path of least resistance. The ladies had gin and orange.

"Let's have some music," cried Alfie, skipping over to the hi-fi. "Here we are, ladies and gents! A spot of the old Twist, as well, eh? Ha, ha. You'll think I'm a bit of a cheeky chappie, what, what?" And a whole lot more, in the same vein. He sounded just like a music hall turn. Molly smiled at me and raised her eyebrows. Thick, dark and unplucked, they were – which rather appealed to me, in fact led me to speculate on the amount of hair under her arms and in the pubic region.

"Take no notice of him, George," she said. "He always gets like this. We only have to have a bit of company and get the drinks out and he starts acting daft."

"Fourteen years of Hell and Purgatory with you'd turn anybody daft," remarked Alfie. "Anyroad up, let's have you, before the record runs off. On your feet everybody! Hup!" He lifted Hilary from the settee and started jigging about in front of her. As I might have predicted, he was a smart dancer. Hilary responded by swaying rhythmically.

"Come on, George," breathed Molly, resting her warm, moist hand on mind, "We're not going to sit out like a pair of wallflowers, are we?" I suffered her to drag me to my feet, and hopped about facing her. Like a good many plump people, she was light on her feet and a graceful mover, but after a while she begged to sit down. I noticed she was breathing hard. Personally, I was glad to leave off my awkward, ill-coordinated jerking.

"Told you to cut down on the starches, didn't I, Molly" yelled Alfie above the music.

"Oh, you! You know it's not that," she moaned.

The record ended and Hilary perched herself neatly on the edge of an armchair displaying her legs gracefully. Although she was my wife only in name, I couldn't help feeling pleased in an odd detached way that she had such an excellent figure.

"Another drink!" cried Alfie. Then, after we were topped-up, "I know what – we'll get the irons out. How's your putting George?"

"Oh, lousy, I expect. I've never played seriously," I replied, hoping he didn't really mean us to go out on the lawn. The evening looked cool-ish by now.

But no, he returned with a couple of putters, golf balls, and a matchbox which he stood on end in the bay. "The thing is to knock the box down. Get it? Then we say you'd have got it in the hole, if you'll pardon the expression. Ha ha." Lewd winks at Hilary and me. A pout of mock-digust from Molly.

We sipped our drinks and putted. Alfie scored about two out of every three. I was little better than the ladies, one hit in a blue moon.

"Hold it, folks! We're not in the right gear. We'll all do a lot better in the right gear!" Alfie dashed out and returned with two cheesecutter cloth caps insisting that we put them on whenever we used the clubs. What idiots we must have looked. Evidently two of the neighbours thought so.- Jane Acres and Ann Grimstock, who stood on their respective drives on the other side of the road, bawling at each other as usual until, when Molly put the lounge lights on, they caught sight of us four cavorting about. They both screwed up their noses and jerked their thumbs in our direction. Pair of old bats! The 'fat gossip' and the 'very fat gossip', I'd always characterised them, to myself. It must have turned chilly because, rubbing their meaty bare arms they took their noisy leave of each other and went in.

"What about a little nibble then, Molly?" asked Alfie. "No, I don't ,mean the old slap and tickle, girl! That's for later." Salacious wink at guests. "A spot of that lovely grub's what I'm talking about. I'll say one thing for my old woman," he added, to us, "where grub's concerned she's a wizard."

Or perhaps one should say – considering her obvious femininity – a *witch*, I murmured to myself. Now there was an idea.

But I'd no time to develop it, for Alfie insisted on showing me his golf clubs which were in the garage. He spent most of his time *insisting*, I imagined. Then, in succession, I had to inspect the bench he'd fitted up, an extensive set of gleaming car tools, and the masterpiece of complexity that lay beneath the bonnet of his even more brightly gleaming Jaguar. His lecture was in full spate when a husky call from the kitchen fetched us in for supper.

Moll's Dad was a butcher, she told me, so they never went short of top-quality meat. Beautiful slices of cold roast pork complete with crackling, a perfect pork pie, sausages on sticks, cubes of ham.

"Good Lord! What a spread!" I exclaimed.

"Oh, Molly! You shouldn't have gone to all this trouble," added Hilary, knowing damned well we had never put on a spread like this for our guests. Not that we'd had any guests for ages.

Supper over, more drinks, more putting, a handful of dirty stories from Alfie, and it was midnight. But the Batterses weren't the sort who let go easily, and we spent a further twenty minutes jawing in the hall.

Alfie kissed Hilary goodnight on the doorstep, and somewhat to my surprise Molly kissed me.

Even at that unlikely hour Ann Grimstock just happened to be putting out her milk bottles.

Naturally, there was a return fixture. The session at our house, also a Sunday evening, was almost a replica. Except that the meats were below par.

Ironically, Molly chaffed Alfie about what she'd do to him if ever she caught him out in any infidelity. This was sparked off by a number of lurid stories in the *News of the World* which Alfie had brought over for my benefit. We all laughed about them.

"But if I ever thought you were playing around like that, Alfie Batters, I'd blooming well murder you!" said Molly, with feeling.

103

"Gerraway! As if I would!" said Alfie.

"You'd better not. I'd... I'd...cut-it-off-with-the-carving-knife!" She brought it out all in a rush.

"Shouldn't do that, Molly,! I put in judicially. "You'd be cutting off your whatsit to spite your thingummy, if you see what I mean?"

"Oh, yes. Ha ha! Quite a wit your husband is, Hilary," remarked Molly, smiling at me. Hilary and Alfie dutifully tittered.

Then Hilary thought she'd break it up by disappearing into the kitchen to titivate the refreshments. Alfie nudged me and pointed to an article in the paper. It was a feature on Surburban Witchcraft, complete with photograph of bonfire in wooded setting and two or three indistinct nudes, all mountainous buttocks and long black hair.

My reaction was one of studied vagueness. Alfie, as always, had his lewd comment to make: "Cor, I bet they don't half do a turn, some of these 'ere witchy birds!" he exclaimed.

"Trust you to be dirty-minded," said Molly. "*I* think it might be very interesting. Oooh, look what it says here. It says 'You never know – quiet, decent neighbours in your own respectable Acacia Avenue may be secret devotees of the booming cult of Witchcraft. "But there isn't an Acacia Avenue round here, is there?"

"It doesn't mean that, you daft ha'porth," explained her husband. "It means just any normal road or street, anywhere."

"Good gracious me! There might be some living along here. You never know."

"Like Bill Hare and Mrs. Wright, you mean? Ha, ha!" Alfie was referring to the cantankerous bald-headed old pensioner who lived next door to him, and an almost equally bald maiden lady who lived in the last house in the Close.

"Too old, Alfie. They'd be nearer our age," I suggested. "In fact, *I* might even be one, for all you know, Molly."

I hugged myself at this audacity, but at the same time my crafty mind calculated that it would provide a useful lead-in if I finally decided to recruit the lady into my own coven.

Chapter 16

'I RAISE my bronzed muscular right arm and She flinches, feeling the lash before it descends. Then, it is her turn. I hand her my forty-guinea bull-hide whip. I cringe on all fours while she stands over me. For my delight she, tall long-legged almond-eyed Minette, wears black lace-up boots reaching to just above the knee, sheer black stockings, shiny patent leather suspender belt, open-crutch g-string and patent leather peephole bra. Despite the kisses I implanted upon her buttocks, belly and thighs in compensation for the weals I raised there, she is bent on revenge. The thong whistles down. A stripe of flame sears the backs of my thighs. By the time she exchanges whip for cane, I'm almost whimpering. She minettes me, true to her name, gobbles me like a sword-swallower till I'm on the brink of orgasm, at which point she cools my ardor with a few neat flicks of the cane. Then the process of excitation again. Then pain. These two, alternately...'

And now, to leave the realms of pulp fiction, and speak the truth:

My arm, white and flabby not bronzed and muscular, was indeed raised... to pour out coffee. The girl is all of thirty-six, plump and homely Molly Batters, respectable housewife and mother. She insists that this is her first infidelity. Far from displaying kinky fun-wear she had on red woolly long-johns over her tights and a bra with dozens of concentric circles of stitching. Her pink crimplene dress had ridden up, and did nothing for her thick waist.

"That's nice," she said, meaning the coffee. "How clever of you to think of bringing a flask. Do you do this for all your girl friends?"

"There haven't been any others," I replied, almost truthfully.

"Go on, I don't believe that. God, I could do with a cigarette!"

"Didn't know you smoked."

105

"I don't, usually. Only after we've...you know. Alfie sometimes lights one for me."

I found this naïve telling of a little bedroom secret a bit irritating, but chided myself. It was simply that Molly hadn't an ounce of guile. I shouldn't allow this to irritate me. After all, the lady had her *good points*. I glanced at them, now decently covered by the concentric stitching, and reflected once again that one could form no idea of how generous they were under her clothes.

Generous was a good word for Molly. For from the moment she'd agreed to 'carrying on' with me she'd thrown herself into it wholeheartedly.

It started on the evening of the Batterses' second visit to our house.

"Come along, Alfie. We'll do the washing up," said Hilary brightly, after supper.

"What? And leave these two alone together?" he replied. "You never know what they might get up to. Still, we'll knock twice and cough loudly before we come in. Ha ha." They left us, shutting the door behind them.

"Oh, he is a devil!" sighed Molly.

"Yes," I answered, scouring my brains for something to talk about.

"What're we going to get up to, then?" she asked in that husky voice of hers.

"Oh..I, er, we'll, we'll go for a drive!" I blurted out. "Yes, I'll take you out for a little spin. We'll only be away a few minutes. Come on, we'll slip out the front. The car's on the drive. They'll not even know we've gone."

I drove much faster than I intended, leaving the village behind me, turning off the main road, weaving along the narrow lanes where, for several minutes, I was lost. We said very little. Then we emerged by a golf course and I pulled into the drive leading to it. No lights on in the club house, no cars parked.

I switched off, dousing the lights also. We couldn't see each other at first.

"Don't you think we ought to go back?" said Molly, a bit shakily.

"Yes, we will. In just one minute," I said. "But first I want to do this." I thought I sounded like some romantic hero of the silver screen, or the long-ago Home Service plays, but unlike those gents I aimed to kiss and missed. Instead I felt her lacquered hair graze my cheek. *She* had more idea than me, turning her head and pressing her lips against the side of my mouth. I found her lips with mine and tentatively nuzzled her. She gave me a warm pressure in return. Then she slowly disengaged.

"Now will you take me back? Please?" she whispered.

"Of course," I said. I drove much more sedately than on the way out.

"Molly, will you let me take you out sometime?" I asked.

"Well, I – I'm surprised."

"Are you?"

"Yes. I didn't think you'd want to."

"Why on earth not? You're, you're a very attractive woman" My clumsy tongue had to grope for the phrases which presumably the practised womaniser uses automatically.

"Get away with you!" she scoffed, but she sounded pleased. "What I mean is, I didn't come across, did I? Didn't give you what you men always expect."

"Oh, Molly. I didn't *expect* anything. I'm not a sex maniac, you know."

"No, love, of course you're not. I wouldn't be out here with you if I thought you were, would I?"

"No, no, you wouldn't. But will you? Let me take you out some evening?"

"All right. If you're sure you want to."

"Yes, I am." We fixed a day and time and place, just before we opened the front door to be met by a gale of derisive laughter and suggestive comment from Alfie. Molly put quite a good face on the matter. For my part, I felt and must have looked more than a little foolish. Hilary wore the incredulous look of one who'd suddenly heard a mouse roar.

107

That was how it began. But things speeded up faster than I could have dreamed possible. Molly was not the sort of woman to play silly buggers, not like Helen Meade and her friend June. Once she'd made her mind up, that was it. All or nothing. She took the initiative, inviting me to pop over on the following Wednesday evening when Alfie would be going to the Works' Club.

I did. She was wearing a tight navy skirt and white blouse, long pendant earrings and about half a gallon of scent. The lounge was a bit too public, so we went into the dining room. I sat in a black vinyl swivel chair and immediately Molly came and sat on my knee.

"Ooooh! I don't know what Alfie'd do if he knew," she tittered. "This is his chair!"

"Oh, I see. Well, how do you know he doesn't get up to something like this himself?" I said.

"Alfie? Oh, he wouldn't. At least, I don't think he would. He'd better not – I'd brain him!"

"But *you're* doing it."

"That's different."

I might have known. She was one hundred per cent woman, was Molly.

After a little preliminary excitation we moved from the chair to the carpet. Molly drew the curtains because we were partly in view from the upstairs rooms of the new houses which had been built at the bottom of the garden. In the greenish twilight we lay locked in each other's arms.

I rolled on top of her but was disconcerted by an irregular banging on the wall.

"It's Denis – you know, Denis Grimstock – he's taking the Hares' chimney breast out." Charming I thought. Just as I'm trying to do ditto with a breast of a different kind. We carried on, but the fuzz of the new carpet was getting up my nose, the infuriating bangs and the thought of what would happen if Alfie came back unexpectedly combined to spoil my efforts and reduce me to winkle-like proportions. Molly tried to keep me up, but it was no use.

108

I apologised, but she re-assured me, soothed away my male humiliation, promised me I'd be all right next time, bless her. Perhaps in the car, out in the country, perhaps. It was enough to make me wonder, in the midst of my gratitude, if this really was her first time. Though I suppose she was just naturally warm-hearted, and practical into the bargain.

In Abbot's Wood under a tree, not far in fact from the site of the last ill-fated esbat, I was indeed all right. We both achieved satisfaction. Molly made me feel good, made me feel like a man. She only marred the occasion slightly by harping upon Alfie's feud with her mother and other mundanities such as the price of children's shoes, the price of meat and the breakdown of her washing machine.

Back in the car, I poured out coffee.

Before we set off for home she asked me if she looked tidy. She'd spent a fair time with mirror, powder and comb, restoring herself to what she'd been when she'd met me down Back Lane over two hours earlier.

"Do you think Alfie'll guess anything?" she asked. "Do I look as if I've been doing...you know?"

"Don't worry, my dear," I said, grinding the gears, "he won't suspect a thing. Unless he sees all those oak leaves sticking to the back of your cardigan."

Chapter 17

THE next time out, I steered the conversation around to witchcraft. Very cautiously, like a subtle salesman arousing interest in his product while concealing the price till the very last minute, I led her on. The plump and delicious Molly I'm referring to, of course. And when a certain point had been reached, at which it would have been psychologically impossible for her to have switched from curiosity to distaste, I showed my true colours. Unless she retracted all she'd said she was obliged to go along with me.

"You've nothing to worry about, my dear," I said in my best Svengali voice. "I shall be there. I shall be with you all the time."

"But what sort of thing will I be expected to do?" she wanted to know. "Nothing horrible, I hope."

"No, nothing horrible. In fact, nothing at all, if you don't want to."

"And what sort of people are they? They're not nasty or dirty, are they? I couldn't stand people who're nasty or dirty!"

"Molly, they're not nasty and they're not dirty. They're just ordinary people. In fact, you know most of them."

"Do I? Who are they?"

"Aha, you must wait and see. What you said the other evening was nearer the mark than you could possibly imagine. Don't worry though, they're all highly respectable. And all as clean as new pins."

An owl hooted. Quite close. Good, it pleased me. So appropriate on this evening.. Tonight... my fourteenth esbat.

(But this *is* where we came in, on the first page. And this event, Molly's Initiation, has already been related).

What I didn't know, that evening, was that she was to be the last initiate.

'The last shall be first' the man said, and so it was with my coven. Molly was the last to come, first to go.

I met her on the day after the ceremony, picking her up in Back Lane, as usual. She was ruffled by the wind and looked rather damp. It had been raining steadily since midday.

"I wondered if you'd be coming," I said as I helped her with the car door. "Rotten evening to turn out."

"I *had* to come," she said, removing her headscarf. She was still panting a little as she fiddled with her hair and rummaged in her bag for compact and comb. "I felt I just *had* to see you." Ominous. I wasn't that irresistible.

"Oh?" I said.

"Yes. Look, George, can we just stop somewhere where we can talk?"

"Well, I thought we could have a drink at *The Forge*. We can talk there."

"No, somewhere more private. Where nobody'd hear what we're saying. Can't you just find a lay-by, or something?"

"All right," I agreed. She said nothing further, though by now I had a good idea of what it must be about.

"George," she said, when we stopped, "I might as well come straight out with it and say ... well, I can't go on with it."

"You mean, you and I?" (Shades of the old Home Service drama creeping up on us once more.) "Or, do you mean the coven?"

"Both, George."

"Both? You, you don't want to see me again?"

"Oh, I don't mean it like that. It's just that, well, you seem a different person to what you were when I met you."

"Different? How am I different?"

"You seemed just a normal sort of man at first. A man who needed, you know. Because Hilary didn't seem to care about you, it made me feel sort of sorry for you. I, I suppose I wanted to mother you a bit."

Good God above! I fairly bristled at this.

111

'Normal'? Me? All my reading of outsiderish literature had convinced me otherwise. To be 'normal' or ordinary, in my book, was as good as being dead! I loved to think of myself as an out-sider figure, a Raskolnikov, a Steppenwolf. How dare this boring little trog housewife call me 'normal'? And as for feeling sorry for *me!* I didn't want anybody feeling sorry for me, thank you very much! Wanting to mother me, indeed! As if I were a little boy!

"Did you really?" I sneered. "And now what conclusions have you reached? That I'm not 'normal'? That you don't feel sorry for me any more, that you wouldn't dream of 'mothering' me?"

"George, please, don't be like this."

"Like what? *I'm* not being like anything. I'm simply...." And then I caught the aggrieved note in my own voice and realised that I was talking to her just as I used to talk to Hilary. Damn and blast and sod it all! Sod her! Sod everything!

I took my glasses off and rubbed my eyes. In sudden weariness I leaned my head against the window. All the windows of the car were steamed up. I had a headache coming on and my neck felt all tense. Depression settled upon me like a black cloud.

My arm registered the touch of Molly's hand. She was peering into my face anxiously.

"George – I don't really want us to – I never really meant that I wanted to stop seeing you. I...."

But I didn't respond. Though I lived to regret it, I shrugged her off.

Chapter 18

I OUGHT to have seen it. Molly was the last woman in suburbia to join a coven. She was just not cut out for it. She was too 'normal', too conventional, unadventurous, and so on. A bit of extra-marital fun was all very well, especially as her smart friend Judy was doing it and boasting about it, but *she* had no time for kinky ritual. Had no need of it. Was frightened of it, in fact. Not surprising really that she dropped out before she'd properly begun.

Once or twice it crossed my mind that I could be enjoying a quiet noggin with her in a nice country pub followed by a spot of what her husband called the old slap and tickle down the lanes, instead of mooching at home. But I didn't mooch for very long.

A few evenings later, about six o'clock, I was out on the drive checking my oil and water when I saw Ron Harvey coming along the Close. Faster than usual, though he normally drove like a maniac anyway. I heard him braking hard on his drive and a slamming of doors, as I wiped my dipstick. It was the only dipstick I had need of wiping these days, alas. Then I became aware of something looming over me. It was Ron.

"That bloody silly git across the road – you heard what she's been up to?" he grated.

"You mean Helen?"

"Yes, I bloody do!" He ducked his head under the bonnet beside me, glancing up and down the road as if somebody might overhear us. "God! I'd like to lower an effing donkey on top of her!" Typical Harvey. Whenever he was niggled by some female then she deserved intercourse with the proverbial donkey, or the proverbial big southern buck, or failing either, with himself till it 'came out of her ears'.

"Why? What's she done?"

"Done? Man, she's done plenty. And she's still bloody doing it! Spilling the bloody beans, that's what!" His pent-up anger actually scared me for a moment, till I told myself not to be so stupid. He could hardly hold me responsible.

"How? How do you know?" I asked. I didn't need to ask what kind of beans she was spilling.

"Look, you don't know Sandra. (I did know her actually, his wife Sandra. She was frigid, fanatically houseproud, clothes-mad and shrewish, amongst other things). She's been suspicious for weeks. Always on at me, asking me where I'm going, asking where I've bloody-well been. Then she goes and hears all this crap that Helen-bloody-Meade's been spreading around, and puts two and two together."

"And makes four," I murmured.

"Don't make a sodding joke out of it! We could be right up the creek without a paddle. All of us, including you!"

"All right, Ron. Take it easy," I said. "What do you really know?"

"Only that that little cowing git's been blabbing to all-and-bloody-sundry." Sulky now, anger evaporated.

"Such as?"

"Such as half the sodding gossips for miles around. All them bitches who go to them coffee mornings, Women's Institutes, and all that cobblers."

"And some of them are friends of Sandra?"

"Don't know about that. But they all talk to her. Because of the parties, you see." Yes, I saw. Sandra was one of the growing army of middlemen – or, I should say, middle-women – who were making a bomb by organising gatherings in other women's homes and flogging ladies' fashion items and whatnot.

"Any names?" I asked.

"Yours."

"Mine? And who else's?"

"Nobody specially."

114

"Oh, marvellous! Well, if you're not mentioned specifically what are *you* worrying about?"

"Bloody hell, man! Sandra! I'm in the bloody doghouse, permanent!"

"Sorry, Ron. But I don't see where I come in. I can't do anything with Sandra." (I certainly couldn't. I did once make a half-hearted pass at her, though I ought to have known better. Glad it didn't come off. She'd have turned me into an icicle the moment I touched her.)

"Almost sounds as if you're blaming me," I added.

"I am. I bloody am! You should never have invited that Meade bitch to start with."

"*I* didn't know how she was going to turn out. Anyway, *you* used to fancy her. You said so."

"Fancy her! Out of spite, man. Bloody spite, that's all." I smiled to myself at this, having got over the alarm I'd felt when he first started blowing his top. I'd heard both sides of the Meade-Harvey bout by now. According to him she'd been a little minx, a scratcher, a biter and an infuriating cock-teaser. According to her he'd been at her like a bull at a gate, all brute force and no delicacy or respect for her as a woman, as difficult to ward off as an octopus in the clinches he'd forced upon her.

Grumbling and groaning, he started to move off.

"What about this Saturday? Can you make it?" I said.

"Can I what? No, I bloody can't!" he replied. "Not this Saturday, or any other effing Saturday. I'm finished."

115

Chapter 19

TWO down. And six to go, could this mean? The expression had crept unbidden into my mind. Though why should it mean anything? Molly was a mistake from the start. Ron Harvey was scared stiff of his missus, and in any case his departure was a major worry lifted from my shoulders.

I told myself not to bother over-much about what Ron had said. After all it was bound to happen. Helen Meade, basically a dull and mousy creature, had to do something to make herself interesting. Inevitably she had begun to hint at herself being a much more exciting person than her public persona suggested. She had put about an idea of herself as being up to all sorts of daring activities. Possibly she had confided, in vague terms, in one or two of her morning coffee friends. Perhaps some good might even come of this: there might even be a new recruit in it for me, some delightful and hitherto unthought-of creature.

"It was that Mr. Whitehouse, that's what Ida says she was saying." My ears pricked up. What was this? Who was this female who was taking my name in vain?

I was searching the shelves of the one and only self-service shop in the village for nothing more exotic than a tin of brown boot polish – unsuccessfully, so far – when I heard this womanish twittering on the opposite side. Peering between the ranks of lavatory cleansers and disinfectants I could just make out two heads, one of them wearing a mannish trilby-type thing with a pheasant's feather stuck in it. Ann Grimstock, who else? And the other, her bosom friend, Jane Acres.

To my disappointment, they launched into a duet on the price of cooked meats and the iniquities of retailers. But then the Grimstock returned to her earlier theme:

"Ida says Helen Meade certainly meant him. Though she didn't so much as mention him by name. Couldn't have been nobody else."

"I always thought there was something funny about him, meself," put in the Acres woman.

"So did I. He's got a sort of, you know, a funny look about him."

"Not all there, if you ask me."

"I've heard his dad was a loony. Been in High Beech for years." The rotten lying bitches! This last one really stung. High Beech was the local mental institution. But it was not even the imputation that my late father had been mentally ill that got under my skin. It was the sheer, rotten, absolute *fabrication of the story.* My father, a Yorkshireman, had never been within a hundred miles of this district in all the sixty-four years that he'd lived!

I'd heard gossip in my time – not that I'd been the target myself, until now – but only at this moment did I realise the bitter truth of the old saying 'If they don't know anything about you they'll *invent* it.'

My father in High Beech! My immediate reaction was to rush round to them and hurl their rotten lie in their teeth. But reason told me to lie low and listen. I listened.

"They say he's clever."

"Thinks he is. Tries to talk clever. But he's only a jumped-up school teacher."

"Now there's a thing. Him, a teacher! Never ought to be allowed. People like him aren't fit to be in charge of young children. Think of it, Ann. The very idea. A person like that being allowed to run around corrupting young minds. Glad mine have left his school."

"Didn't you say your Colin did well in his class?"

"Oh yes, Colin did well. But he would, wouldn't he? He's a clever lad, is our Colin."

You stupid cow! I muttered. Your Colin, clever? He was a nice enough lad, but he could just about write his own name when he came to me. By the dint of extra attention and bags of encouragement I raised him from being positively backward to being 'fair' 'Fair' was

117

his limit.

"Makes you wonder how long it's been going on," said the Grimstock.

"What's going on, Ann?" Since breaking off for a quick dote upon her youngest son, Acres had lost the thread.

"You know – the orgies. These 'ere witchcraft goings-on."

"Ah, yes. Well that Helen Meade good as said she's in the thick of it. And there's about a dozen of them all told. All in Horton Drive and Shrewsbury Avenue, would you credit it!"

"What sort of things do they do, like? Did she say?"

"Well, Dorothy – you know Dorothy, next door to Ida, no, Dorothy Hines I mean – she says Mrs. Meade says they do ritual dancing in the, you know."

"Naked, do you mean?"

"Yes, that's it. Disgusting!" I felt inclined to giggle at this. Were it not for the malevolence in their voices and the realization that this sort of talk, if it got about, was going to cause a mighty lot of trouble for me, I'd have found it hilarious.

"And there's *sacrifices,* they say," continued the Grimstock. "Yes. Ugh! Makes my blood run cold! They kill cats and roast them on altars. And chickens…"

"How vile! And offer them up to the devil, I suppose?"

 Well, yes, they're bound to, aren't they?"

"How awful! In this day and age, and in a Christian country. Not that I'm much of a church-goer myself, but I think that's simply horrid. It's … it's…."

"Blasphemy! It is! They ought to be dealt with like they was in the old days! Burned at the stake!"

"I don't know as I'd go that far. But I suppose you're right."

"There's a sight too much of this kind of thing going on!"

"Semi-detached Satanists."

"You what?"

"It was in the *News of the People* last Sunday, this article about them. 'Semi-detached Satanists' it called them.. All living in a respectable London suburb and secretly they was witches."

118

"Like this lot. We're respectable round here – all nice houses – yet there's this wicked lot carrying on under our noses. Could understand it if they was from the Council Estate. But to come from among decent law-abiding ratepayers, it makes my blood boil!"

I noted the rise in the Grimstock's blood temperature. It had been running cold a minute earlier. The lady gave a snort and moved off towards the way out, Acres following.

I hung about for a moment till I thought they'd have finished with the cashier, and then came out of hiding. But they were still there, chewing the fat down by dog foods and deodorants. Acres saw me and nudged her, even fatter, friend. They both tossed their heads and threw their baskets-on-wheels into top gear. In haste to get away from the leper, I supposed.

True, I reflected, as I went on searching for the boot polish, we did live in semis, all of us. It was only the 'Satanists' label that didn't fit.

Then, with a start of alarm I realised that there were people who would *make* it fit.

A couple of days later I saw some more of them at it. This time I was in no position to eavesdrop, as it happened in Horton Close. Three of them, three gossips, standing about halfway along the road, two of them with shopping baskets, the third leaning on a broom. I was mowing my pocket-handkerchief of a front lawn and with each alternate mow I could see them, wagging their bottom jaws up and down and looking at each other and then every so often at me.

I recognized them. One was Ida Harkness. She was about 43, had one daughter, Merril, an elephantine child whom she insisted on dressing more like a boy than a girl. Foolish, because the poor child was a bit butch to start with. Besides her was her old crony Dorothy Hines. About the same age, different kind of daughter. Hers was a pretty girl, slim and very feminine. These women were identical in two respects: both had trim, expensively-clothed bodies, both had malicious lying tongues. The third was a woman who kept to herself, usually: Teresa Rolls. She was in her early thirties, had a boy and girl,

119

helped with the Wolf Cubs and was, so Hilary said, a puritanical Catholic. She, more than anybody, would be bound to be horrified by the lurid tales which the other two were undoubtedly feeding her.

I could just imagine their accusations. Drunken orgies, devil worship, sacrifices, lustful perversions, boiling up toads in cauldrons, flying on broomsticks. You name it, they would be saying it, smearing, accusing, condemning. The lying bitches! Three more rotten lying bitches whom I could cheerfully murder!

One of these three surprised me, though.

Shortly after I'd finished my chore I heard a tapping on the garage doors. I was at the bench, trying to put an edge on the shears with an old file, and it must have been this ghastly teeth-jarring row that told whoever it was that I was in there. Who the devil could it be?

I turned the Yale and opened the door a few inches, a degree of caution befitting one who might expect to be led away to the stake or at least the ducking-stool at any moment.

"Mrs. Rolls," I said, surprised.

"Mr. Whitehouse. If you could spare a minute?"

"Yes, yes. I'm not doing anything special."

"Well, I'll be telling you straight. That's not what *I've* been hearing," she said, coming in and pulling the door to behind her.

"What do you mean?"

"I'm meaning, Mr. Whitehouse, that there's folks around here that're saying you've been doin' all manner o' things."

I sighed. "I saw Mrs. Hines and Mrs. Harkness talking to you."

"They're not the only one, Mr. Whitehouse. There's others in this village who've got it in for you."

Ah. So, she's not one of *them*. She's actually come to warn me!

"Why?" I asked. Might as well find out what I could.

"Because, because they say you're a Satanist, that you're a monster, that you're God-knows-what. There now, I've told you."

"Hmmm. And do you believe them?"

"Sure I'd take anything them two say with a large pinch of salt."

120

"Good, I'm glad to hear that."

"But there'll be something in it, I'm thinking."

"Oh?"

"So you'd be well advised to be careful, Mr. Whitehouse."

"I will. But why are you telling me all this, Mrs. Rolls?"

"I'm telling you, because to my way of thinking these evil tongues is worse than anything you might be doing, whatever."

"Yes, gossip is a terrible thing, Mrs. Rolls."

"It is that, an evil and a powerful thing, Mr. Whitehouse. Powerful it is because you can't fight it. But I've said all I wanted to say. I'll be taking my leave of you."

"Thank you, Mrs. Rolls, thank you. I didn't think there was anybody like you in this road. I thought they were all the other sort."

"You'll be right there, Mr. Whitehouse. They are."

She went. And I returned to my filing in sober mood. The grating of the metal was an apt accompaniment to my thoughts. I was thinking of the evil tongues. Not only the harsh, ugly sound they made, either. It was their fickleness. Last week it was X who had a naughty illicit thing going with Mrs. Y. Now it was me.

Chapter 20

INEVITABLY, Hilary got to hear. She put it to me obliquely, to begin with. We were just finishing dinner.

"George? Are you feeling all right?" she asked quietly.

"Me? All right? I'm fine. Why shouldn't I be?"

"You've been a bit odd lately."

"How?"

"Oh – far away, living in another world. You've been out late, quite often. 'Course, it's none of my business where you go or what time you come in. I couldn't care less."

"Well, what are you on about then?" I challenged.

"As I was saying, I couldn't care less, except for the fact that I've been hearing things."

"Have you?"

"You're in some kind of trouble, aren't you?"

"Hazard of the profession."

"What's that supposed to mean?"

"School teachers, scout masters and clergymen – the three traditional targets for the arrows of scandal."

"For God's sake, stop talking like a book!"

"Nearly as bad as Terry Welch."

"Go on, if you must. Who's he?"

"Who *was* he, we should say. Alas, he is no more. No, not dead, but worse. Dishonoured! Odd that I never told you about him."

"I remember now. You did. The fellow who cheated in the 11-plus, told his kids the answers."

"He did more than that. Surely I told you about the other business? About him interfering with girls?"

"Good God, George, no! That would be the end. You haven't...."
"No, of course *I* haven't. I'm not a criminal! I'm not another Terry Welch. (I paused to relight my pipe) It was quite a business, old Terry. He got the sack for it, naturally. The first I heard was when I was working in the Library with six of my girls, third-year Juniors I had at the time. They were supposed to be helping me with cataloguing, but we were chatting away, slacking off really as it was just coming up to break. I happened to be saying something about Welch. I forget what it was, when one of them – Christina Bass, Anglo-Indian girl, beautiful child, clever too – interrupted me with 'Mr. Welch is rude.' I wondered if I'd heard correctly, but one look at the other girls' faces told me I had. 'Rude? How do you mean, rude, Christina?' I asked her. She wouldn't answer. But another girl, Anna Andreyevitch, piped up with, 'He puts his hand up the girls' dresses.'

'He does *what?*' I said. I nearly hit the roof! 'What on earth do you mean? Which girls?'

'The girls in his class, sir.'

'Hm. Sounds like a lot of nonsense to me. Where is this supposed to happen?' I was trying to pooh-pooh it, you see, but I could tell straight away that it was a case of no smoke without fire.

'At his desk, sir.'

'At his desk? You mean in front of the whole of 4A?'

'Yes, sir. He did it to Maria Murphy yesterday, sir. She told me, sir.'

'Good God!' I exclaimed.

'Oh Golly! I'm not letting him do it to me!' squeaked Eileen Casey. Little dot of a child, she was.

'That's enough!' I said. 'This sort of talk is very dangerous. Now listen to me, you girls. Don't go flapping your mouths all over the school about this. I'll look into it, that's a promise, and I'll have a word with Miss Gould. (Miss Gould was the Headmistress.) If you girls are foolish and don't take my advice then you could make a lot of trouble. And some of it could be for yourselves Right? I know you can be sensible. And I'm sure I can trust you.

123

"Huh!" interrupted Hilary. "Trusting ten-year-old girls to keep their mouths shut? Talk about an optimist! But this has got nothing to do with you, George, with *your* trouble."

"I'm coming to that. Well, my advice did no good, because the whole business blew up, on that same day. Within half an hour, in fact. My class was being taken by a student, so I had another free period after break. And I was just on my way back to the library when four or five girls from Welch's class came clumping up the stairs like baby jumbos. 'Where do you think you're going?' I said. 'You can't see Miss Gould. She's very busy.' But they were round the corner by then and knocking on the Head's door. I hung about to see what'd happen. I heard her call 'Come in' in her plummy voice, and in they all trooped. The door closed and I couldn't hear any more."

"Thank God for that! Now can we get to the point?" demanded Hilary. I'd noticed that she was getting more and more impatient, and was enjoying it.

"I had the full story at twelve o'clock," I went on, ignoring her, "when the old girl sent for me. 'Mr. Whitehouse,' she said, all breathless, 'do sit down, please. A terrible thing has happened, a thing I never dreamed could possibly happen to mar the happiness of my school, er, of our school, that is. Mr. Welch...I... oh dear, this is simply awful! Mr. Welch – he's in the hands-of-the-Police! And he's suspended from all duties in this school!' She was rather embarrasssed to begin with, but I suspect that she is beginning to get a kind of shivery thrill out of it. It appeared that Welch had been up to his old tricks during the morning, and had tried it on with the wrong girl, a girl called Linda Burton. She was a rough type, very troublesome, but she'd got guts. She called him a dirty old man, and dragged four of the other girls, presumably those who'd been interfered with, off up to the Head's room.

"Gould phoned the Chairman of the Managers, Father Worthington. I told you it was a Roman Catholic school, didn't I? Then she phoned the police, and the Education Officer, in that order. Result was that by noon Welch'd been hauled off to the nearest cop-shop and a police-

124

woman was interrogating 4A girls in the Medical Room. Christ, what a schemozzle!" I paused to relight my pipe.

"Good heavens! How revolting! What a nasty little story!" said Hilary. I chuckled. She looked furious with herself for being interested.

"That's nothing," I added. "You should have heard, or rather smelt, the stink raised by the parents! And when the local gutter press got hold of it – God, did they make a meal of him!"

"I've no doubt they did. But, George – am I ever going to get a straight answer from you?"

"You mean what's the point of telling you all this stuff about old Welch?"

"Yes, I do!"

"Because I'm in nearly the same position myself. Except with me it's not molestation of children".

Hilary sat quite still for a few moments. Then she took a packet of cigarettes from her handbag and asked me for a light. I guessed this new habit was connected with Alfie, but made no comment.

"I don't suppose it's much use asking," she said wearily, "but what exactly *have* you been doing, George?"

"Well, I've, er, formed a kind of little group. Er, a society."

"To do what?"

"To study, er, ancient rituals, medieval ceremonies, that sort of thing. Historical, you know."

Her eyes widened. "So, it's true!" she gasped.

"What's true?"

"All I've been hearing! You're, you're a leader of a group of so-called witches! All the perversions and blasphemy and vile behaviour really are going on!"

I boggled. The change in her was startling. No less startling was the fantastic turn of feminine logic whereby the admission that I belonged to a group automatically confirmed all the accusations levelled against me!

125

"There's no harm in it, Hilary. We do none of the things we're supposed to have done," I protested.

"How do *you* know what they say?" she snapped. I explained what had happened in the shop, what the Grimstock and the Acres woman had said.

"Disgusting," said Hilary.

"I agree. They should have been strangled at birth, the pair of them."

"*You*, I mean. It's *you* that's disgusting!" cried Hilary. Again, I received a jolt. There was no doubt about her horrified expression.

"It's nothing like that. We're more like, kind of, scholars," I protested.

"Rubbish," said Hilary, curling her lip. "Nobody learns that sort of stuff in schools. Unless you've started preaching your particular brand of filth to your pupils? That's what they'll be saying next, believe me!"

"Hilary, it's all nonsense. I...."

"Stop it, George. Don't bother to give me any more lying excuses. Don't say another word. I've had quite enough of the subject!"

"But let me explain. Let me try to make you understand...."

"I understand all I need to, George. No, no, don't tell me (holding up her hand like a policeman) I've only got one thing more to say."

"What?" I asked dully.

"That I utterly wash my hands of you."

Chapter 21

THE coven seemed to be grinding to a halt. Apathy, apathy, all around me. I wasn't exactly ablaze with enthusiasm myself, but I knew that unless I galvanized by followers into action the whole thing would fizzle out. At best (no, cancel that – at worst) I would find myself alone with Buttercup and Poppy once more.

Opportunity presented itself in the shape of Maurice Clundon tinkering with his car, futilely as usual. Without bothering to light my pipe I stuffed matches into my cardigan pocket and went straight out to him.

"Evening, Maurice, ..."

"Oh, it's you," he said. "You're the very last person I want to see!"

"Really?" What the hell now, I wondered.

"Yes, really! The bally balloon's gone up with a vengeance! Fleur's furious!" This combination of cliché and tongue-twister struck me as being diverting, but not for long.

"Your wife? What does she say?"

As if I couldn't imagine it. She would explode, but oh so genteelly. Fleur Clundon's affectations were one of the standing jokes of the neighbourhood. Everybody, even newcomers to the village, picked up the story of how she'd started life in humble circumstances, with her fair share of the local accent, and how she'd become 'refeened'. Her first step up the social ladder had been her association with Maurice. Her going to 'electrocution' lessons had followed hard upon. Even today, her every sentence was marked by the same painstaking observance of non-existent aspirates as in w*h*y and w*h*ere, and the never-to-be-exorcised fear of lapsing into the dreaded Midland vowels.

127

She had a part-time secretarial job, but believed it to be a closely guarded secret, it not being quite the thing for a JP's wife to go out to work. She had a number of hats of chamber pot design, and instead of wearing them it would be truer to say that she walked along under them.

"She's furious, absolutely livid!"

"Oh? Is she?" My air of vagueness and incomprehension would have done credit to the village idiot, if we'd had one.

"She feels that she can no longer hold up her head as a member of the Church Social Committee. And what's more she's threatened to resign from the Drama Group. She says she's open to, to Public Ridicule!"

"But can't you reason with her, find out what...."

"How can I, man? Damn it all, *she's gone*! And she's taken Peter with her!"

"Good lord!"

"Yes, back to that little hovel where her mother lives."

"Oh, Lord."

"For God's sake stop calling on the Lord, Whitehouse! If *you'd* been a Christian, all this would never have happened. There'd have been no hocus-pocus, no gossip, and no wives leaving home! It's all your fault. You're a menace to the community! Will you kindly go away and leave me in peace!"

Chapter 22

I COULD hardly blame Clundon for being a bit hostile, I suppose. Typical of him that he hadn't really got down to the root of the matter. But he didn't need to tell me, I could guess. The gossip originating from that stupid Meade bitch and spreading like ripples on a pond, had implicated him, and had eventually reached Fleur. He had lost his local squire image, his wife, and Goofy, his son, at one fell swoop.

So, he was out of it.

I must have been extremely dim, but I never visualised the gossip spreading to the one place where it might make things awkward for me. That is, to my employers. I don't mean the big shots up at County Hall, but the local small fry.

The first I heard was when the Head buttonholed me for a confidential word as I arrived on Monday morning.

Norris Whittaker was a fairly typical Primary school headmaster. Fair organiser, adept at handling parent problems, just about coped with sorting out the timetable each September, prodigious writer of smarmy duplicated bumf for the kids to take home, mediocre teacher. No real intelligence, culture minimal. He'd been at the school fourteen years, two years longer than myself.

"'Morning, George. Nasty morning. We'll not bother to hold Assembly this morning – they'll get too wet walking over to the Hall."

"Right," I murmured, anxious to get my keys and escape.

"Ah, George. There is one small thing before you go. You'll never guess what nonsense I've been hearing." Jocular. Could be anything. Anything but you-know-what. I waited.

"I had some stupid woman telling me the most laughable thing."

129

. " Absolutely fantastic. Said she'd heard somebody saying that you're the leader of a secret society or something, that you're a proper Jekyll and Hyde. 'Course I soon put her right. 'Look here,' I said, Mr. Whitehouse is one of the most dependable members of my staff. Always has been. Tower of strength. What you've been saying about him, I told her, is about as likely as one of Her Majesty's Government turning out to be a crook! (Not a very good choice of simile, to my way of thinking.) Ha ha!" brayed Whittaker. "All I could do to stop myself laughing in her face!"

"Ridiculous," I snorted. "Some women are capable of retailing any sort of story, however impossible it might be."

"Just what I thought, George. The birdbrained creature actually said – you'll never credit this – that you were the head of a witches' coven! Unbelievable!"

While Whittaker was delivering himself of these last few words Ethel James, school secretary, came into the room. I left at the same moment, so I didn't know whether she'd noticed what was being said or not. She'd have something to say if she had, because she commented on anything and everything in the bluntest and most tactless way imaginable. For this reason and because of the way in which she guarded the school stockroom, most of the staff called her 'the dragon'. But she wasn't a bad old stick, in my opinion.

On the Tuesday morning it was a different story.

"Whitehouse, I want a word with you," was all the greeting I had from Whittaker. No 'George' this time, I was 'Whitehouse' with a vengeance. Gone was the jocular, all-good-chaps-together tone of voice. Instead he spoke in a hushed intense manner, how I imagined a bank manager would talk if he'd caught one of his cashiers taking home samples.

"Yes?" I said.

"Yes, indeed! I must say I'm absolutely staggered. Staggered and horrified! I would never have dreamed that a member of my staff – that any member of the profession, in fact – would have got mixed up in

130

such a disreputable business!"

"What business?" I asked. I'd never liked this smarmy, pompous ass Whittaker, and although I knew damned well what he was on about I was determined to make him spell it out.

"Oh, this dabbling in... you know perfectly well what I'm talking about, Whitehouse... this witchcraft tomfoolery."

"Tomfoolery, eh?" I said. "Well, if that's all it is, then it'll be quite harmless, won't it?"

"Not for a man in your position, by Jove. Not, at least if you have any proper respect for   your professional status,   for your,   your responsibilities, your, er, place in the community." Oh, bollocks to the 'community', I muttered to myself. I was fed up to the back teeth with the wretched word. It'd suddenly become the catchword of every damned conversation.

"My advice to you," he went on, "and I hope to God you'll take it, Whitehouse, is to cut out this funny business. Right away. Drop it, man, drop it, and keep your fingers crossed that all these rumours die a natural death."

"Nothing to drop. There never *was* anything in it. Just a   few harmless games inspired by some silly talk at a party. It was a dare, that's all. Simply a handful of friends, fooling about. Strictly for laughs."

"I'd like to think that was the truth. My goodness, I certainly would!" He stood there shaking his head with disapproval and wearing a nasty-smell-under-the-nose look, as I went out.

Reaction amongst the staff was negligible. I could tell that they knew, by the artificiality of their talk. They could tell that *I* knew *they* knew by the extreme brevity of my remarks, in contrast to my normal fake garrulousness, and by the glances I kept darting at them. The staffroom atmosphere was a trifle strained. But nothing to what it was going to be, as time went on.

The only person who made any direct reference to the situation was Miss James. I went into her office to ask about certain items of stock.

131

But she ignored my question.

"They're being absolutely stupid, Mr. Whitehouse. I shouldn't take any notice if I were you," she said quietly, looking up from her typewriter.

"I don't, Ethel. I don't take a blind bit of notice of them. In this job you always get some silly mother complaining that you've been shouting at her little Johnny, or some such rubbish."

"That's not what I meant," she replied. "I'm talking about these accusations of witchcraft."

"Oh?"

"Yes. And I think the staff's nearly as bad as these gossipping parents."

"Are they?"

"Well, they're just shaking their heads and passing on the rumours, instead of quashing them."

"Probably they think it's all true. Mr. Whittaker seems to think so."

"Pooh, him! Doesn't know whether he's coming or going, that man!"

"You know – you're the only person who's not convinced that I'm a witch."

"Huh! You couldn't be, could you? Witches are women."

"You're not quite correct there, Ethel. Men can be members of groups who practise witchcraft. There's probably as many men as women involved in it."

"Oh, you're thinking of the sort of thing they write in the Sunday *News of the People*. But anyway, you could never be one of them."

"Hmmm. I'm very grateful for your faith in me, Ethel. Makes me wonder how you'd react if you thought what the others think. What'd you say if you knew that I really *was* mixed up with witches?"

"Huh! The very idea!" She slipped a fresh sheet of typing paper into her machine. I watched her while she tapped out date, addresses and 'Dear Sir'. Then she looked up at me over her glasses.

"I'd have very little to say, unlike most folk. It's my opinion that as long as a man does his job properly, if he's a good teacher, as in your case, then what he does in his private life is his own affair."

132

Chapter 23

"HOW are things in the world of witches?" sneered Hilary at the breakfast table.

I had slept badly, had a splitting head, a mouth like the inside of the proverbial Turkish wrestler's jockstrap, and felt in no mood for conversation of any kind – let alone having the mickey taken out of me.

"Bollocks," I muttered, sugaring my tea.

"Not so much fun now that the beauty of your little circle's abandoned you, eh?"

"What bloody beauty?" I snorted, stirring with unnecessary viciousness.

"Why, the glamorous Annette, of course."

"Annette who?"

"Hamlyn, you idiot. The sex kitten of Shrewsbury Drive. One of your lady witches."

"Huh, her!"

"Mmm. Disgruntled, aren't we? Didn't come across, did she? There, diddums. Should teach the little man not to set his sights so high. Should stick to the little plump-homely-housewife variety. Models and actresses are not really in our line, are they?" Sneer, sneer.

"Bollocks."

"Really, George! What a limited vocabulary, for a self-styled culture-bug. Anyway, you've lost her. However little you got out of her, you've had it."

No response.

"Mind you, she was clever. She made out that she only went for a lark, just the once, that she didn't really get involved." That was true enough. There was only one thing that women like Annette Hamlyn

133

would ever get seriously involved in. And that was their own bright, brittle, shallow, selfish lives.

"Whitehouse, there's something I must tell you. And I want you to think very carefully about it." This was Whittaker, ponderously grave, a week after his outburst of righteous disapproval.

"Yes, and when you've given it Earnest Thought, I hope for God's sake you'll make the Right Decision – the *only* decision, if you're thinking straight. The fact is that I've received a number of demands for your resignation. Some by letter and some by telephone. I must warn you that I am bound to pass them all on to the School Managers."

I sighed, "What do you want me to do?"

"There's only one Proper Course. Write out a letter of resignation to the Managers, copy for the Education Committee, copy for your own reference. Then you should look for a job elsewhere.

I was sleeping badly. Very badly. Some nights I only got three or four hours. I had almost constant headaches. Probably these last were due to the terrible rages I worked myself into, in the wee small hours. I would get out of bed and pace up and down in my dressing gown and slippers. It was God-knows-how-long since Hilary and I had shared a bedroom, let alone a bed.

I would rant and rave under my breath, rehearsing over and over the searing, blistering phrases that I would use on my enemies, phrases which would utterly annihilate them. I would lapse into bouts of self-pity, bewailing the fact that the whole world was against me. That there were exceptions, like Teresa Rolls, and now Ethel James, counted for little. They were merely two isolated dry patches in an overwhelming flood of hostility. At times I would align myself with those witch-martyrs of the seventeenth century, persecuted by a harsh and repressive regime. But I drew no comfort from this either. My mind was a treadmill.

On nights like this I tried to escape from myself by reading. Until I discovered Music I'd been an omnivorous reader.

Now, at 3 a.m., I knew that sleep was impossible. So I pulled on a dressing gown, went downstairs, and settled myself in front of the electric fire with a pot of tea and the biscuit tin.

I thought of reading, but was too apathetic to go to the bookshelf. I knew what I'd find there. My latest half-hearted gleanings from the Mobile Library: Crime Club, spy thriller, two vaguely sexy novels. Fundamentally unsatisfying. Disbelief in them couldn't be suspended long enough. Their shallowness and falseness to life kept breaking through at every turn.

At last I forced myself to grab a book. It was a Penguin Modern Classic I'd picked up on a railway station and never opened. Hermann Hesse, *Narziss and Goldmund.*

Though I distrusted such phrases as 'strange friendship that grew up', 'their bond', 'their high destiny', referring to the association of the two young men, I began to get interested in the book. I'd read Hesse before, and though I admired his style and skill had tended to dismiss these friendships of his, always between two youths, the one intellectual and masterful, the other more sensitive and vulnerable, as being perverted and sick. I mean that I'd thought Hesse a bit sick in drooling over them as in *Unterm Rad (The Prodigy)* and *Demian.* But I could not dismiss his insight, especially his grasp of the motives and behaviour of his background people.

You might be forgiven for thinking this a bit of my old self-conscious culture-bug flummery, as derided by Hilary, but it has relevance. It rings true, anywhere, anytime, this observation of Hesse's about background people. It's like that with *my* background people. Not on so refined a level as in Hesse. But only let those scum who live around here get their hooks into, say, a couple who've got something going between them, like X and Mrs. Y a month ago, or hear of anybody who's got a passion for anything above their feather-brained heads, like poor old Z painting nudes, and the whispering campaign gets under way, the poison tongues go to work! Let them just have the faintest suspicion that somebody's on to something pleasurable and they're jealous as hell. They hate him, or her.

And now they hate me.

And whose bloody fault is it, I asked myself as I stared blearily into my cornflakes next morning. That sodding Meade bitch! My God, she was due for a sorting-out, and no mistake!

It was nearly a week before I found an opportunity to have a go at her. I'd just got back from my school and she'd just got back from the shops. Fortunately for my purposes, she didn't stay in the house unpacking her shopping like any normal housewife, but immediately re-appeared on the front with leather and duster and began cleaning her lounge windows. I left my pipe on the window-sill and marched out of my front door. She didn't notice me until I was standing at the foot of her stepladder with my chest on a level with her ghostly-white legs.

"Helen – I've got something to say to you," I began.

"Have you really? Well, I don't think I've got anything to say to you, George," she replied. The coy, sickly-sweet tone of her voice made me want to slap her silly face. Or, as I hadn't a hope of reaching that, one of her whiter-than-white calves.

"No, but you've had plenty to say elsewhere," I snapped. "You've been blabbing your mouth off all over the village, and making trouble for me, haven't you?"

The anger in my voice must have chipped some of the varnish off her, because she sounded nowhere near so bright when she replied.

"I don't know what you're talking about," she said. With which classic rejoinder she came down her steps and tried to escape into the house. I grabbed her arm.

"Hang on a minute! You don't get off as easy as that, I haven't finished all I've...."

But at that moment Jim's car swung into the drive. He got out heavily, a pile of school exercise books under his arm and briefcase in hand.

"Let me go," hissed Helen. "I'll tell Jim about you hurting my arm..." "He's about as pleased

"He's about as pleased with you as I am, I should think!" I hissed back.

136

"Hello, my love," grunted Jim. "'Lo, George. How's it going?"

"Not so good. Bad, in fact. And I hate to have to say this, Jim, but it's largely due to your wife!"

"Don't listen to him, darling," cried she. "He's come over here and attacked me. He's shouted at me. And he's hurt my arm!"

"Nonsense!" I snorted.

"I say, that's a bit thick," mumbled Jim. Old sheep! Doubt if he'd do more than mumble 'that's a bit thick' even if he caught me raping his missus on the front lawn!

"Look, Jim," I said, "you ought to get a grip of Helen. She's been spilling the beans around the coffee parties (ha ha – joke, I don't think!) Everybody knows about the coven, and who's in it."

"I've done nothing of the sort!" she squeaked. "He's lying, Jim!"

"She's a menace to all of us," I said, "to you as much as to me, Jim! Haven't you had any gossip filtering back to you?"

"No, er, I can't say as I...."

"Well, you will, believe me. Could affect your career. And you'll know who to thank!"

"Hum. Don't know about that...."

"It's all his fault, Jim," squeaked Helen. "Don't you let him set you against me. Just think – if he hadn't talked us into that business in the first place, there wouldn't have been any trouble. We never really wanted to join anyway, did we, darling?"

"No. Er, no, that's right. All your fault, George. So, er, don't come over here attacking my, er, wife."

"All right. I'll leave your, er, whatever she is, alone!" I sneered. "But I'm extremely doubtful about including either of you in future activities of the coven."

"Don't worry yourself," cried Helen haughtily. "We wouldn't dream of getting mixed up in anything so sordid again!"

They scuttled into the house, and I stumped back to my own house, hands in pockets, in a filthy temper, aiming a vicious kick at the Harveys' cat as I came upon it sniffing around my dustbin.

Chapter 24

DONE for. Washed up. The end of the coven. I examined the suds in the bottom of my beer glass, and reflected that my creation, the product of my drive and imaginative genius had come to a similar end. Only the lees left.

But I'd not reckoned with the potency of those lees.

I was in the mobile library, with a couple of straight novels in my hand (no occult rubbish nowadays; I'd done with all that) when I felt something grip my elbow. By the feel of it through my suit jacket it should have been the talons of a vulture, no less. But it was Aggie. She gave a jerk of her head and tugged at me. I allowed myself to be led down to the far shelves.

"Tomorrow night," she said in a hoarse whisper. Her greasy ringlets brushed my cheek. The reek of Californian Poppy nearly knocked me over.

"What?"

"Tomorrow night. If we miss it we'll have to wait a whole year for it to come round again!"

"Miss it? Miss what?"

"The Rite of the Un-dead. Surely *you* should know, better'n me or Jen. You're the scholar, ain't cher?"

"Yes, yes, of course I am." I replied warily. Though perhaps if I'd been more wary, and less of a conceited idiot, I'd have denied that I'd ever heard of such a Rite, challenged its very existence. But as it was I had to go and put on the old infallibility bluff, thinking to consult the books, and then go one better, as usual. I wish to God I hadn't!

"You be round at my house, half-eleven tonight."

"What about Sid?"

"He'll be at his Club, boozing. Not be home till one or two in the morning. Jenny'll be there. She's been missing you, you know." Leer, leer.

No, I didn't know, and I didn't care. Even if she had an overwhelming letch for me, which I didn't for one moment believe she had, I didn't care. As for her mother, she sickened me. Revolting old bag! How I'd ever allowed myself to. Ah well, that was in the past.

My immediate reaction was to say, 'Bugger off, I'm finished.' But then I changed my mind. If I hoped to reform the coven, with new, more carefully-selected members next time, new, more gratifying women especially, then I'd need a nucleus to begin with. And, as witches, Buttercup and Poppy were at least genuine. Indeed, they were the only true believers. They could be used in the future 'to encourage the others', as it were.

"I'll come," I said suddenly. "Make all the necessary preparations for the Rite," I added, trying to sound authoritative.

"Oh, don't you worry yourself. I'll do that," breathed Aggie.

As I left the mobile library I glanced at my watch. Still only 4.15. I didn't normally leave school till nearly five. Hilary *would* be thrilled to see me come home early.

Halfway along the Close what should I see but the bread van of Freddie Osborne parked on the drive, my drive. He was in the house with Hilary. Something else for the neighbours to talk about. Ah well, it might take their minds off me for a while.

I debated whether to knock, or cough loudly, before going in. But of course I did neither. It's ridiculous, the idea of knocking on one's own front door. I dumped my briefcase in the hall and went into the lounge.

There was Hilary, reclining elegantly in one chair, showing her legs right up to her backside, smoking. In another, perched on the edge, looking very awkward with an unaccustomed cigarette, was Freddie. I thought I could detect something of an atmosphere.

"Ah, greetings, Frederick," I said breezily. He looked even more awkward, if that were possible. I'd taught two of his daughters, both

139

extremely pleasant girls. He stood somewhat in awe of me, I felt on account of my being 'eddycated'. Village bobby tongue-tied in presence of village schoolmaster, as per nineteenth century. I mused. Though I always chatted lightly to him, trying to put him at his ease, it only seemed to make him worse.

"Well, I'll be, er, getting along," he mumbled.

"All right, Freddie. Byesie-by, then," said Hilary sweetly. Bloody bitch. Freddie was welcome to her, I thought. A moment later he drove off, with much loud revving-up as if to let me know he was a good driver even if he wasn't a very fluent talker.

"Naughty, naughty," I said to Hilary, wagging a facetious finger in her face, "Little wifey carrying on with the tradesmen behind hubby's back, eh?"

"Oh, that," she replied absently. "It was finished ages ago. He was trying to make a come-back."

"And you turned him down?"

"Naturally. He's not the only pebble on the beach. In fact, he's not even on it any longer."

"No, he wouldn't be. We're rolling around with a much bigger pebble these days, aren't we? Flashy Jaguar, cigars, smart restaurants, boxes of chocolates, etc. We've come a long way from the bread man."

"He's a Special, as well," put in Hilary, irrelevantly, as I thought, completely ignoring my jibes. "He's just been made up to Sergeant."

This reference to Freddie's other career proved to be not quite so irrelevant from my point of view, the way things were to turn out.

"Where've you bin?" screeched Aggie as she let me into her hall. I frowned at this. Hardly the kind of greeting I expected, as High-priest. "Quarter to bleedin' twelve!" she went on. "I said to be here at half-eleven. We'll be late!"

"Plenty of time," I said. "It doesn't take me fifteen minutes to get my robe on!" I looked at Jenny and raised my eyes to the ceiling as if to say 'your mother's off her rocker.' But she too was scowling.

"For Gawd's sake!" she hissed. What a little hellcat, I thought, seeing

140

the mean look on her cheap nasty little face. What a bloody pair, in fact! There was nothing to choose between mother and daughter.

"What the devil's the matter with you, both of you?" I snapped.

"Nothing. Nothing at all!" said Aggie. "It's just that we've got to get ready, and then it'll take us about ten minutes to *get there*. And we've got to be *in position* on the stroke of midnight."

"Where, for goodness' sake?"

"Ah, I knew you didn't know the Rite! Imagine it, Jen, teacher hasn't done his homework. The churchyard, that's where we're going, George. The churchyard. So don't bother to take yer shoes off. Now, we've got to be there by midnight, so get a bleedin' move on! You as well, Jen, get yer coat on top of that lot."

Aggie already had her bit of catskin on over her robe, and was wearing the inevitable wrinkly white plastic boots. Jenny put her bit of nylon mink on top of her mini-robe. She had ditto boots, except that they were black. Between them they bundled me into the lounge.

In high dudgeon I removed my clothes and put on my robe. When I re-appeared in the hall only Jenny was there.

"Ma's getting the car started."

"Thought Sid would have taken it," I muttered.

"Not him. Likes his booze too much. Gets 'is mates to pick him up. Come on, she's ready."

"Wait a minute. I can't go out like this!"

"Oh, put this on, then!" She whipped a rather expensive-looking camel coat off the hallstand and threw it at me. Lord, I thought, Sid dressed a hell of a lot better than we poor impecunious schoolmaster types.

We scrambled into the car. I sat in the front, Jenny at the back. Aggie flashed a sidelong glance at me.

"Jesus Christ, our Jen!" she yelled over her shoulder. "What d'you want to go and give 'im yer Dad's coat for?"

"Why, Ma?" asked Jenny sulkily.

"'Cos it'll make things awkward later on, you daft little git! That's why!" I didn't follow. Surely Sid's coat would be back on its peg

141

before long. How would he ever know I'd borrowed it?

Aggie's anger made her driving even more erratic than it was to begin with, and I found myself stamping on non-existent brakes at every corner.

We pulled up into the little lane beside the village church and got out, closing the doors quietly. Aggie led the way to a corrugated-iron roofed shed which nestled in the shadow of the east end of the church. She pulled open the rickety door and dived inside.

"'Ere, take this, George," she whispered.

"Good Lord!" I gulped. A spade!

Before I had time to protest, they took one of my arms each and frog-marched me along a gravelled path that ran down the south side. There was a light breeze. The thin spire, quite clear in the moonlight, seemed about to pierce a solitary cloud that hung behind it. I could even see the moss on the tombstones.

"Here," said Aggie. "Got the stuff, Jen?"

"Yes, Ma."

"Give us it, then."

Jenny produced what I thought for a moment were candles. She gave one to her mother and thrust one into my hand. Then I knew what it was, though I'd not handled the stuff since my days in College dramatics. It was greasepaint.

Jenny and her mother had thrown their coats open, lifted their robes, and were drawing cabbalistic signs on their bodies. I half-heartedly began to copy them. Aggie was not satisfied. She went for me with her stick of greasepaint and drew rapidly on my legs, belly and chest. I didn't like this one little bit. Damn it all! I was the High-priest! It was *I* who was the leader of the coven, the brains of the outfit, not some half-baked illiterate housewife!

"That's enough," she said. "We've no more time. Get digging!"

Jenny snatched the spade and started attacking a grass-grown mound like a maniac. After a moment her mother pushed me forward, took the spade off Jenny, thrust it upon me and galvanized my arms into the action of digging.

142

"Dig, for Gawd's sake! Do it quick!" she said.

"But, but, we can't just dig up bodies, just like that," I protested feebly.

"Pooh! Bodies! There'll be nothing. Only a few bones, if that!" scoffed Aggie, squinting at her wristwatch.

What the blazes? This obsession with time was beginning to get on my nerves, on top of all the other rigmarole. Barmy, the whole lot of it. Where the devil she'd dug this rubbish up from, I couldn't imagine. There was nothing in Idries Shah about it. Nor in any other book I'd ever read.

"Stop!" cried Aggie dramatically. "We're doing it all wrong! The book says quite clearly that robes should be folded three times and laid behind us."

Reluctantly, I took off Sid's beautiful camel coat and folded it, lining side out, before laying it on the grass. Then I put my robe on top of it, folded three times, as Aggie insisted. All I had left on were my shoes.

I stood shivering with cold and indignation, glaring at them. They hadn't removed their own coats, the bitches! Some Rite, this! Specially designed so that *I* had all the hard work and all the discomfort as well!

Just then the clock in the tower struck, nearly making me jump out of my skin. Only the one dull, metallic boom, that's all it ever chimed, on the hour.

"Dig, O mighty Felix! Dig as fast as you can!" exhorted Aggie. Jenny tittered.

Oh, God! What a farce! In sheer bewilderment and rage I savagely drove the spade into the soft ground and levered up a few clods.

Then I heard the crunch of a footstep on the path. Where the devil did those two bitches think they were going? I spun round furiously.

It was then that I got a nasty shock. A torch shone in my face.

"Now then, sir, what's going on here?" said a voice. Christ, no! The Law – in the person of Freddie Osborne!

I looked in vain for Aggie and Jenny. They'd vanished!" I groped around at the edge of the path. My robe, and Sid's coat, also vanished!

143

They'd taken them, the bitches! *They'd* dropped me right in it! The rotten, treacherous bitches!

"It is my duty to warn you, sir, that anything you say will be taken down...." began Freddie, in a style copied from the telly.

"Don't be daft, Freddie. It's me, George Whitehouse," I interrupted.

"So it is. Well, I'm sorry to find you mixed up in this here disgusting business, Mr. Whitehouse. I was warned by telephone that there'd be some grave-robbers up to their tricks tonight. But I never thought to find you were one of 'em."

"But I'm not! Look here, Freddie, this is all nonsense. It's not grave-robbing. It's ... it's all just a lark, er, a bet, I'm only doing it for a bet! My friends are all hiding behind the tombstones. You'll find them if you look. They, er...."

But Freddie just stood there shaking his head in point-blank disbelief. I tailed off into silence.

"You're committing two offences, you know, Mr. Whitehouse: unlawful opening up of graves, and also hindecent exposure. I should by rights take you down to the station."

"Oh, my God! But you wouldn't, would you? Think of...think of (inspiration hit me!) Think of Hilary. You wouldn't want to upset Hilary, would you?"

Freddie said nothing for a moment. Then he shook his head ruefully. "No, no I wouldn't," he said. "So I reckon I'd better not have seen you. And you'd better shovel that earth back and then get off home as quick as you can, Mr. Whitehouse." Still shaking his head, he turned his broad back on me and stumped off.

"But, I've no clothes!" I wailed after him.

"Can't help that, Mr. Whitehouse," he replied over his shoulder. "You'll just have to manage as best you can."

I was fairly dithering by now. And absolutely livid. My only hope was the shed. I hastily scraped the few spadefuls of earth that I'd removed back into the hole and went to put the spade away. All I could find to cover me was an old smelly sack.

144

I felt absolutely miserable and terrified as I crossed the main road outside the church, wearing only my best brown shoes and the sack. It was a nightmare – like those nightmares I'd had as a boy, in which I used to run through the streets in my Chilprufe vest with my little willy hanging out and everybody laughing and pointing at it. Only this was worse – it was true!

The street lamps were still lit. My only course was to cringe along on the inside of the pavement, ready to dive into the nearest gateway if I saw anybody. Soon I had to do this, as I spotted the headlights of an approaching car.

Three-quarters of the way home, another car appeared. Again, I leapt into somebody's drive.

But unluckily the front door opened at the same moment and two elderly women came out. They froze in the middle of their goodnights when they saw me caught in the light from the hall.

"Really!" exclaimed one of them.

"Go away!" shouted the other.

"Yes, go away before we call The Police!" screamed the first. I slunk out through the gates.

"Disgusting!"

"Must be drunk!"

"Must have come from one of them there drug-taking parties!"

These and other conjectures followed me as I hurried away.

Then it dawned on me that I couldn't get into the house! No keys. They were in my clothes. I'd have to go to Aggie's.

And, by God, I'd do something to her! I'd never in my life struck a woman, but I was damned well going to strike one now!!

I padded along Shrewsbury Drive like a hunted animal. Aggie's windows were ablaze with light, the curtains undrawn. And there in the lounge, puffing on a big cigar, was Sid!

Oh Christ, what was I going to do now? Obviously I couldn't knock on the Uptons' door. My only hope was to go home and see if a downstairs window had been left open. I always closed every window religiously myself, but Hilary might not have bothered. If it came to

145

the worst I would have to spend the night in the garage.

I made it home without meeting anybody else. No windows open at the front of the house. Waste of time trying the front door, the Yale would be on. I tried the garage door. Open, thank God! I stumbled upon something. Reached down and felt it. My clothes!

With something like a prayer of thanksgiving, I let myself into the house. I cleaned myself up in the kitchen, though I didn't manage to remove all the greasepaint, and crept into my lonely bed.

Next morning I found an envelope at my breakfast place. Hilary had picked it up in the porch. It bore only my name and the words 'By hand'. I slit it open, and read:

Felix,

It is our decision that you have failed in your sacred duty as High-priest. Your introduction of such unsuitable persons as that Primula, you know we mean that Hamlyn woman, into our midst is all the proof we need that you are lacking in true reverence for The Craft.

We hereby EXCOMMUNICATE you.

Signed, Buttercup, High-priestess.

Poppy, assistant priestess.

P.S. Do not attempt to make further contact with us. And, be warned! Do not attempt to practise The Craft ever again, or you will Surely Be Punished!

Chapter 25

"HERE you are, George, another little billet-doux", sniggered Hilary. "I didn't know what the last one was about, naturally, as you know I wouldn't dream of opening your letters. But this one, I do. It's from another of your lady-witches, the charming Mrs. Meade, this time."

"Charming, my arse!" I muttered. It was breakfast time, only twenty-four hours after my 'excommunication'. "What the blazes is it? I haven't got my glasses," I grumbled.

"I'll get them for you, my dear," cooed Hilary in a tone of maddening mock-sweetness. She was back in a second, and put my spectacles-case down beside my cereal dish.

Now I could read what was on the orange booklet she handed to me.

"Oh, for goodness' sake!" I groaned, "the Parish Magazine? What do I want with this?"

"More than you'd think. Helen said the Vicar's newsletter should interest you."

"Like hell it will," I said and turned to the inside of the front cover.

PARISH CHURCH OF SAINT STEPHEN AND ALL HALLOWS

A message to our parishioners from your Vicar, the Rev. Hugh Somerhayes, M.A. (Cantab.), B.D.

My very dear Friends,

It is with great sadness that I have to record the death of Mr. William Robinson, at the age of 81, last Thursday at his home in Malthouse Crescent. Mr. Robinson was for many years a sidesman here at Saint Stephen's, and he...

(I skipped a few lines)

...efforts of the Mother's Union whose Bring and Buy Sale raised the princely sum of...

(this wasn't it, either)

...disturbing and insidious new feature of Suburban life...

(Ah, this was it! Backtrack a little).

It is with great regret that I have to mention the fact that a certain disturbing and insidious new feature of Suburban life has begun to rear its ugly head even here in our charming little village. I am referring to the current vogue for dabbling in occult matters, such as the practice of 'witchcraft'. No doubt there are people who have read lurid accounts of the so-called modern 'covens' in certain sections of the national press. Irresponsible and crudely sensational accounts, it must be said! These people feel that they would like to dabble in such matters themselves. But such dabbling, my dear friends, can only lead to moral degradation.

I would be failing in my duty as your Pastor, my dear friends and parishioners, if I did not warn you against the evils of such practices. In our modern 'out-for-kicks' society where the sense of right and wrong is so often in abeyance, it is we Christians who must stand firm. It is we who must set the example. Above all, friends, it is we who must pray for our brethren who have fallen by the wayside.

Let us put our trust in Our Lord Jesus Christ, who in his mercy is ever ready to stretch forth his hand even unto the most hardened sinner, that those in our midst who would incline towards evil ways shall speedily forsake them.

That these people may be otherwise sober and respectable members of our community makes the whole business the more regrettable. Let us even more earnestly, my brethren, address ourselves to prayer that their repentance may be happily accomplished.

Yours, in Christ Jesus,

Hugh Somerhayes.

148

"Huh! Holy Hugh! The benevolent beanpole. Most amusing I'm sure," I muttered.

"Extremely well put, I thought," said Hilary. "He's right, you know."

"You think so? Well why don't you do as he says, then? Get down on your knees, woman, and pray for the poor sinners," I jeered.

On the Friday of that week, it occurred to me that I'd be seeing the beanpole himself, in person. It was the Harvest Festival service in the school hall and Somerhayes had been there to conduct it every year for as long as I could remember.

But for once he wasn't there. He was away at a clergymen's conference, and we had to make do with a stand-in, the Rev. Peter Sandiland, minister of the village Baptist Church.

He was very hard to read, this Sandiland. A smoothie, of indeterminate age and un-pin-downable views. Though at least I must admit that he didn't talk down to the kids in quite such an obvious way as the vicar.

It was his words in the staff room rather than his words in the hall which niggled me.

He stood by the mirror stealing a quick glance at himself, just enough to smooth back his already immaculate wings of silvery hair, sipping his cup of tea almost as genteelly as Fleur Clundon would have done.

"Thank you, thank you, my deahs. So kind," he said caressingly to the female members of staff who were waiting on him hand and foot and crooked elbow. "Excellent spot of tea, most excellent." For crying out loud, I thought – he made it sound like vintage champagne.

"Most happy occasion, this, for me, Headmaster," he said, turning to Whittaker. "Indeed yes, all those smiling faces, happy innocent faces. You know, when I look at young children, I always feel, that is, I say to myself, how can anyone doubt that God's in His Heaven, and all's right with the world?"

What a load of balderdash! Surely he must know what lies behind those angelic expressions? Innocent faces? They're little devils! Not all of them, of course. But quite a few, especially those who look as if

149

butter wouldn't melt, etc. They're the worst.

"Ah me." Sandiland exclaimed, setting down his cup and saucer. "Pity the *world's* not so innocent a place. You know, Headmaster, I've never in my life composed a sermon remotely resembling the one I prepared for last Sunday. No, never, as far back as I can remember. Mind you, you may say, that I'm 'preaching to the converted', and when I think of the good people who come along to Chapel I'd have to agree with you. But somewhere a voice must be raised. Even if it's only raised in the presence of the righteous, instead of directly in the face of those to whom it applies. Yes, I firmly believe this; a voice should be raised.

"Why, I was saying to Mrs. Sandiland – my wife, you know - only yesterday, how alarming it is that this pleasant little community with which we've been associated for so many happy and fruitful years should lie under such a blight. I'm speaking, my deah Headmaster, of this outbreak of so-called 'Satanism'. You've heard talk, of course?"

Whittaker coughed and spluttered and spilt tea down the trousers of his Harris-tweed suit. The faces around me looked embarrassed. All eyes found a sudden, unaccustomed interest in the bookshelf or the educational magazines on the coffee table. All avoided me as though I were something nasty on the carpet whose presence it would be unmannerly to acknowledge.

"Er – yes, yes, Mr. Sandiland. Yes, er, people do talk, in a small, harumph, place like this."

"Indeed – but can one blame them? That is what I would contend. Can one expect the ordinary man in the street, the housewife, the mother, the average law-abiding upright member of our community to forbear? One sees evil, one comments. It is inevitable, is it not? Though whilst condemning evil we should of course not cease to pray for those enmeshed in it. That goes without saying.

"Ah yes, we should be on our guard. Ever on our guard."

Amen. A-bloody-men! I thought bitterly. Of all the beastly audacity. To come out with this snidey, oblique condemnation while I was actu-

150

ally in the room! It was no accident. He couldn't *not* know about me, that was impossible. Ever on our guard, indeed! Why? Why bother? No need for him or any of his pious crew to guard themselves against contamination. They'd – but, wait a minute... I couldn't be more wrong. One of 'the fallen' was in fact a leading member of *his* flock. Maurice Clundon! Lay-preacher, Treasurer of the Chapel Social Committee, star of the Drama Group. How on earth could I have forgotten that? I felt quite bucked. It'd be a feather in my cap if I could recruit a few more for the coven from amongst his congregation. The thought of several of those po-faced bible-thumpers tripping around a wicked bonfire in the buff, enthusiastically led by Mrs. Sandiland herself, put new heart into me. I'd get back at him, the swine! I'd turn every Baptist in the village into a witch!

But then I returned to earth from my megalomaniac visions. I knew that I'd never get even one of them. The hunt was up, I had to admit, as I filed out of the staff room door with the others, glaring at Sandiland's back as Whittaker escorted him to his car. The rats had all left the sinking ship (I didn't give a damn about mixing metaphors if they served), and now there was only me left on board.

Having read the beanpole's epistle, and now having heard smoothie Sandiland on the subject, I ought not to have been too surprised at the third Christian sect in the village taking fright.

But I hardly anticipated that battle would be joined on my home ground.

It was therefore with something of a shock that I saw a dog-collared gentleman turn into my drive and march up to my front door. I'd been engaged in my usual sport of leaning on the lounge window sill, smoking, whilst I surveyed Horton Close, when I first spotted him in the distance. As he drew closer I saw the Roman collar. He began peering at house numbers.

We were actually staring at each other, separated only by a pane of glass, when he pressed his forefinger against the bell push. I couldn't pretend I was out, so I had to go to the door.

"Yes?" I said, not taking my pipe out of my mouth.

"You'll be Mr. George Whitehouse." Statement of fact, rather than question, I noted. Broad Irish accent, and mad eyes, flaring nostrils, I also noted.

"Father Michael Mallon. I'd like to come in for a moment." No hinting about this, no salesman's ploys. It was a direct, no-messing request. I didn't see how I could refuse.

"Right. But I'm rather busy."

"So I noticed," he said, shedding his raincoat and dropping into an armchair opposite me. None of the 'may I sit down' pussy-footing of the C of E curate who'd once called. Being a priest he was so used to going into people's homes he just treated them as his own, I supposed.

"What can I do for you?" I said, urbanely.

"Y'r on my Register, so ye are. Y'r a Catholic." He pronounced it 'cat-lick'.

"No, no, there's some mistake."

"You were put in the Parish Register – 'tis there in Father McManus's own hand – when ye first came to live in the Parish. 'Twas twelve years ago." It was true. Like many another, ahem, ahem, intellectual, for example, Auden, I'd flirted with Catholicism briefly.

"But, Father," I said, "that's a long time ago. A lot of water has – "

"Once a Cat-lick, my son."

"But I've not been, it's been years since...."

"Since ye've been to Mass, since ye've been to the Sacraments (he pronounced it 'Sark-a-ments') Ah, the times I've heard it, the old, old story."

"Wait a moment," I said. "Why is it that you've allowed me to lapse all these years? Why are you now so anxious to save me?" As if I didn't know the answer.

"There comes a time in a man's life, my son, when he's walking on, like, a knife-edge. On the one side there's God and Our-Holy-Mother-the-Church, and on the other, the Divel. And once a man starts to lean, to lean, like-you-know, towards the Divel's side, then he's on the brink of Eternal Damnation." (and Hell-fire, I added mentally) "Now, from

152

all I've been hearing, ye've got a powerful strong leaning on yiz at the moment."

"Why don't you spell it out, Father?" I put in. "I wouldn't expect a priest to talk in riddles like a C of E."

"No call to go criticizing Our Separated Brethren, my son. And I don't have to be spelling anything out. Y'know perfectly well that I'm talking about this damned witchcraft!"

He fixed me with an intense look, sat waiting for me to answer. I wavered. If I'd had enough natural authority, enough presence or personality, I'd have sent him packing. Part of me wanted to go for him, ask him how he had the audacity to come into my house, accusing me. But I knew I couldn't do it. There must be something in the old malarkey about the backing of the mighty Roman church with its two thousand years of experience, its authority derived from J.C. himself, its intellectual storm-troopers like the Jesuits and Dominicans – something of all this force behind even the humblest backwoods curate – because I felt he had the measure of me, with plenty of spare. I retreated into the same spiel that I'd given Whittaker.

"...and that's all there was to it...," I ended.

"Right. I'll hear your confession, then," said Fr. Mallon briskly.

"Oh, no – I, er, that is, my views have – "

"Well, I've no time to waste. You'll know where to come. At Our Lady of Perpetual Succour confessions is at 11 to 12, 4 to 5, and 8 to 9, Saturdays, and 6 to 7.30, Wednesdays. Make y'r peace with Almighty God, my son. Ye'll be a lot happier. There's no happiness outside the Faith, y'ought to know that!"

"No, no, I'm not.... It's not my cup of...er, not any more...."

"I'll pray for ye. In fact I'll make it the Intention for 8.30 Mass tomorrow. Now I'll leave ye in God's hands. I've to draft out a bit of a sermon, like – warning the Faithful against the divelry that's going on. And I've to *asperge* a certain place in the wood by Parson's Lane. You'll know the spot, I don't doubt."

"No, I don't know it."

"Well, y'ought to. Because it's you and your gang of hellcats that's

153

been lighting bonfires there and treading the earth down in a ring with your dancing."

How damned stupid can you get? I said aloud as I closed the door upon the departing Fr. Mallon. I knew the spot he'd mentioned, of course. And I also knew that it was a favourite playground for kids from all over the village. Everybody knew that kids went in there and lit fires. I could just imagine the priest spraying holy water around, thinking he was purifying witches' territory, when really it was territory belonging to cowboys and injuns.

Speaking of cowboys, I saw a group of them whooping down the road, firing off cap-guns, as I got my car out on Sunday morning.

Only, one of them was dressed wrongly. Instead of chaps, revolver and stetson, he wore a big flapping thing like a cloak. As they stopped outside Helen's house (her boy Martin was one of them) I could see that there were signs on the 'cloak'. Cabbalistic signs! Good God – *my robe!*

I walked, as though casually, past them. When I was close to the boy wearing the robe, I said, "That's a fancy cloak you've got there."

"'S mine," he said, wiping his snotty nose on the sleeve of it.

"'E found it," volunteered young Martin, "down among some bushes in the churchyard."

Chapter 26

THE gossips must have done their work well. Everybody seemed to know about me by now. People stared at me quite openly.

At the shops, on the following Saturday morning, the feeling of hostility was unmistakeable. I saw looks of distaste on the faces of the quiet, reserved types; dismissive shrugs from the more wordly, who obviously thought I was some kind of nut-case; I could even hear jeering remarks from the Dorothy Hines and Ida Harkness variety. All sorts of other, unexpected, people had things to say. The following is a sample, these being remarks passed by a considerable number of people, standing about in groups of two and threes:

"That's him!"

"The devil!"

"Is it true what they say, then?"

"Is it true? I'll say it is! And it's my belief that we haven't heard the half of it!"

And, a little further on:

"Vile!"

"Disgusting!"

"He looks a quiet enough fellow…"

"Ah, they're always the worst."

And outside the hairdressers':

"I don't know why he's been allowed to continue in his job."

"Mrs. Grimstock says she saw them all, especially him, *at it,* when she was out walking the dog."

"How horrible!"

"Yes. Dancing and sacrificing dumb animals and so on."

"My neighbour's cat's disappeared."

155

"That's nothing!   My brother-in-law's missing half his chickens!"

"It's that devil! He's sacrificed 'em!"

By the newsagents' and tobacconists':

"He's split up marriages, they say."

"All the women are pregnant!"

"No...!"

"Yes. They've sworn an oath to breed children and baptize them into them into the service of the Devil."

"Ugh! Wicked!"

Amongst the timber off-cuts and plastic buckets outside the D.I.Y. shop:

"Sticking pins into people, an' all."

"Pins? Into people?"

"Well, images, you know. Dolls. They stick pins into dolls to make people ill, their enemies, like..."

"They've made the Vicar's wife ill."

"They've murdered an old tramp."

"And eaten him!"

"Horrible!"

"There's no end to what they've done."

"What *he's* done, you mean!"

And, outside the chemists's:

"Some of them have given it up, they say."

"Ah, but not *him.* He's swore a pact with Satan, so I've heard. He'll never give it up. And he'll get more new ones to join."

"Ought to be drummed out!"

"Will be, the way things are going!"

So much for the jeers that I heard or, in some cases, fancied I could hear.

Then there were the fool tricks played by kids.

156

I was on my way into the Post Office when I heard giggling behind me. It was a trio of silly girls, about eight years old. The second time, I swung round in time to catch them pulling faces and making rude signs. They did exactly the same when I came out again, five minutes later.

Then there was one incident where a child was actually put up to it by his elders.

Two men, about the same age as myself, nudged each other as I walked past, and one of them whispered in the ear of a young lad who was with them. Both men chuckled, and the lad got the giggles. I ignored them and walked on trying to look unconcerned.

But I'd not gone far before a guffaw made me turn round. The lad had a besom broom, which he must have grabbed from the stand outside the garden shop, and was riding it hobby-horse fashion behind me! When I glared at him, he rode it back to where it'd come from. Quite a number of people saw this. They either sniggered or looked down their noses in disgust. Though the disgust was, I felt sure, at me rather than at the lad.

When I got back to my car, I found that some unknown artist had decorated one of the door panels. Traced in the dust was a crude picture of a witch on a broomstick.

I was seething with anger as I switched on the ignition. But by the time I'd reached home and was making a cup of tea I began to experience a new sensation. For the first time, I began to feel actually afraid.

The headaches seemed to be getting worse. I lay awake for long periods in the night. On three, or even four nights of the week I seemed to be downstairs brewing up endless pots of tea, smoking endless pipesful of tobacco. I'd had to change to a cheaper brand, I was smoking so much. My nerves were definitely taut. The backfiring of a car one evening nearly frightened the life out of me. When I stepped on the bathroom scale I was astonished to find that I'd lost about half-a-stone in a fortnight.

The old brainbox didn't seem to be functioning very efficiently, either. I received final demands for bills I felt sure I'd paid. Couldn't seem to

157

balance my school dinners register without adding the columns up several times over.

This last was the cause of my doing something I immediately regretted.

I'd got a real dose of the Monday-morning blues, had had another bad night, stuffed-up feeling from a beastly head cold, felt about ninety-five years old and wished myself anywhere but in the schoolroom. To add to this the children were more than usually fussy. There'd been a sudden downpour just as they were all on their way to school and the wet coats and steamy windows made me even more depressed. I stared in dismay at the column of dinner money and the pile of cash on my desk which just wouldn't agree.

Two girls were whispering. "Shut up and get on with your work!" I shouted. There was peace for a moment. Then the same two began to point at somebody else's work, and make signs. I shoved back my chair and marched over to them.

"I've warned you two...." I said. I could feel my temper on the point of snapping.

"Sir – it's David. He was showing us his drawing," said one of them. I was all set to blast her for trying to drop another child in it to save her own miserable skin, when the picture caught my eye. It was a very artistic piece of work, but it's subject made me see red. It was *a wizard*, in conical hat and star-patterned robe!

"You cheeky little monkey!" I roared. "This is meant to be me, I suppose!" And, completely losing control of myself, I slapped him on the side of the face. His eyes opened wide in disbelief before they flooded with tears. The rest of the class stared in horrified silence.

With shaking fingers I picked up the offending piece of paper. There was a piece of lined paper with it. On the top line, in beautifully neat writing, it said: 'Book review. A Wizard of Earthsea, by Ursula le Guin.' Numbly I remembered how I'd enthused about this book, how I'd purposely given it to this particular boy to read. With a sudden access of shame I realised that I'd struck the last child in the whole class to deserve it – David, my best pupil.

158

Chapter 27

I HAD an awkward time of it explaining to Mrs. Bonser, David's mother, how the incident had occurred, how it was all a mistake. I ate humble pie in great chunks. I explained that I'd not been well, and offered to go round to see Mr. Bonser, who normally got home from work very late. Mrs. Bonser said that wouldn't be necessary, in the end.

I tried to explain to David himself, wondering if I'd ever regain his confidence.

One thing the incident did do, was to confirm my suspicions that I was going to pieces.

Far from dying a natural death, as Whittaker put it, the rumours seemed to be hotting up. Though it seemed to me that they could hardly reach a more scandalous pitch than they had done already.

Yet, the anti-George campaign, unknown to me, was about to enter a new and more militant phase.

An envelope arrived for me, marked 'URGENT. PERSONAL', addressed in block capitals. I found that the letter inside was also printed in capitals. There's no point in reproducing it here. Suffice it to say that it was illiterate in style, abusive in tone, and marked by a profusion of dirty words and wild, unfounded accusations. I threw it straight into the waste bin.

It was not the only one. Two more followed in quick succession. Neither appeared to be in a disguised hand. Nor was either of them as abusive as the first. Both, I would say, were written by women.

The letters did not worry me over-much. But the phone calls did.

I picked up the receiver one afternoon, giving my number as usual, and found a very nasty customer at the other end.

159

"Home from school, are yer?" Hoarse, uncouth voice, might have been a man *or* a woman, I couldn't tell.

"Who is it speaking?" I asked.

"Never you mind, *mister* Whitehouse." Definitely menacing tone, sneering emphasis on the 'mister'.

"What do you want? Look here...."

"No, you look, mister! This is just a little warning, like. We're on to you, that's all. We know all about you."

"What on earth do..." I began, but the line went dead.

I've always been rather impressed by this kind of scene when I'd watched it on the telly. The anonymous caller, the threats, the feeling of impotence on the part of the victim – it'd always seemed convincing. Now I knew why. Because this is just the way it happens. Only, I wasn't an actor saying his lines. I really was the victim. And, just as in the plays, I knew he'd call again.

Next evening.

"Hello? Hello?" I gave my number again.

"Still there, eh, Mr. Whitehouse? Not flown off on yer broomstick to one of yer wicked orgies?"

I didn't bother to reply, I simply slammed the receiver down. Half an hour later it rang again. I didn't answer. Thought about calling the police. But I was hardly in a position to call upon *them,* especially after the business with Sgt. Freddie Osborne.

Next day, at five o'clock, I had another call.

"They'll be round to fix yer."

"What ? What do you mean?"

"That's all, they'll be round. Tomorrer night. But we'll not say what time. We'll keep yer in suspense, like."

"Wait, wait! I – hello?" He'd gone.

Hilary came in just before midnight, from wining and dining with Alfie Batters I didn't doubt. I felt I had to talk to somebody, so I told her about the calls. As I might have expected, she wasn't very sympathetic

"All nonsense," she said. "Just some crank – the sort of person who gets a perverted pleasure out of making anonymous telephone calls. Probably somebody not all that different from you, George."

"Do you mind! That's a rotten thing to say. This maniac who's ringing up is not even remotely like me. He's uncouth and clearly of low intelligence."

"Then there's not much to worry about, is there?"

"On the contrary, he sounds highly dangerous. Don't forget he's threatened some violence for tomorrow night!"

"Violence, my foot. People who make those sort of phone calls aren't violent types. They'd probably run a mile if anybody challenged them."

I saw that there was a certain amount of wisdom in that, though I didn't draw much comfort from it.

"You may be right," I said doubtfully.

"I shall be out again," Hilary said, "but if anybody attacks you, you have my permission to hit him with one of my saucepans."

I could not settle to anything. The goggle-box only irritated me. My library books failed to hold my interest. Even my pipe refused to burn properly. Involuntarily I kept looking at my watch.

Eight.. eight fourteen.. eight twenty-seven.... I observed the passing of all sorts of odd hours. Nine fifteen, and I decided to put a record on the hi-fi. It was Mozart, the G minor symphony, 'this fatalistic piece of chamber music' according to Alfred Einstein, quoted on the sleeve.

I listened with perfunctory attention to the first movement, it being somewhat spoiled for me by having its opening theme cribbed for a pop record. Then the second movement grabbed me by the scruff of the neck. How those unlikely demisemiquaver pairs, repeated ad nauseam (or would have been in anybody else's hands) manage to generate such emotion, is nothing short of a miracle. I shut my eyes and felt a shiver in the nape of the neck such as I hadn't felt since the almost-forgotten moments when I was besotted with music, years ago.

But I didn't get to the end of the movement. A terrible splintering crash jerked me out of my chair. Lying on the carpet, amid jagged shivers of glass, was a half-brick.

Chapter 28

I WAS shaking when Hilary arrived home. She came into the lounge to find me standing in the bay window, with the room in darkness and the curtains drawn back, staring out into the Close. The beer glass in my hand was empty, as were the two quart bottles I'd bought at teatime.

She switched on the lights, making me blink like an owl.

"What on earth have you been up to?" she asked, eyeing the piece of hardboard I'd tacked up at the window.

"Somebody threw a brick," I muttered.

She sighed. "There you are – you see what you've brought upon yourself." A silly remark, but at the same time maddeningly true. My predicament, plus the beer, suddenly washed over me, so that I began to wallow in waves of self-pity, and not for the first time. I resorted to the familiar mixture of feeble rage and maudlin regrets. I'd been a fool to think that I might exercise my imagination, do anything different from the mediocre norm, in this community of boring, bigoted imbeciles. For all their fridges and TV and cars, they were the eternal *peasants,* the same mindless sheep that one would have had to contend with a hundred years ago. Or, *three* hundred years ago, in the days of Matthew Hopkins. I should have known that I couldn't do what I had done and hope to get away with it.

I recalled the time before I'd embarked upon my career as a witch. It now seemed positively desirable!

"I don't suppose you'll be staying," I said, observing Hilary as she lit a cigarette.

"You what?"

"You'll be going home to 'Mummy', won't you?"

163

She looked surprised. "No. Why should I?" she said, closing her green shadowed eyelids in an affected way.

"Well, it won't be very pleasant for you here, with this sort of thing going on."

"It doesn't affect me really. After all, it's *you* they're throwing bricks at, not me."

"But you've had a phone call from the maniac, as well."

"Oh, that. I don't suppose *I* shall have another. I just told him he was being a silly schoolboy. And he actually apologised, said he thought he was talking to you."

"But what if you're sitting here some evening when a brick comes through the window, like tonight?"

"It's not very likely I shall be sitting here, actually," she replied. "I go out rather a lot, or hadn't you noticed?"

At school, I merely went through the motions of teaching. I couldn't summon up the slightest enthusiasm. The whole place seemed as drab and miserable to me as, well, the inside of my own mind. I don't know what kind of man my pupils were seeing, or my colleagues. But if my outward face was any reflection of my inner feelings then I must have presented a ghastly picture.

The school was in a delightful setting on the fringe of the village. The children were as likeable as one could find in any school in the country – but the sight of the meadows, the farm on the hillside above, and the sounds of laughter from the busy playground merely served to mock me, lost in misery and depression as I was.

One afternoon, just as I was telling my unfortunate pupils to 'get on with the next exercise' – a travesty of my former style of teaching – the Head came in. He had somebody in tow.

"Ah, Whitehouse," he cried, with his usual mock-heartiness. "We have a visitor this afternoon. Mr. Wheate has just become a Manager of the school, and I'm giving him a, you know, conducted tour of the place."

Wheate came towards me. I recognised him. He'd been at Annette's

164

party.

"Mr. Wheate has two children in the school, Helen and Philip," added Whittaker.

Wheate's hand was dry and firm, much larger than mine, with long muscular fingers. He didn't try the 'grip like a vice' that some oafs affect, but I had the feeling that he could have pulped my hand with the greatest of ease if he'd wished.

"How do you do," I murmured congenially

Wheate did not make the stock reply, but merely nodded slightly. He had rather peculiar eyes, almost black, and a very direct way of looking at you.

Whittaker blathered on for another half minute, about how lucky we were to have Wheate as a Manager and so forth, then they departed.

As the afternoon dragged on I found myself thinking more than once what an odd fellow this Edmund Wheate was. I was quite surprised when I recalled that he'd not spoken a word, either to the Head or to me.

When the evening of the P.T.A. Annual General Meeting came round I didn't feel in the least like going. But in the end I did.

I'd been very active in the P.T.A. until a few months previously, and was a retiring member of the committee. In fact, it was on this very point that the trouble arose.

The meeting was sparsley attended as usual. Apart from the officials, there were only about twenty parents present. Very poor, considering there were over 200 children on the school roll.

I was intrigued to see Wheate sitting in the front row. Though I might have known he'd be there in his managerial capacity. I thought I caught him looking at me intently, once or twice. I wondered what he was thinking.

We listened to the usual tarradiddle from the Chairman, a smarmy vote of thanks from Whittaker, and the Treasurer's Report. You can imagine the boring predictability of it all.

Then came the *un*predictable.

165

Whittaker was listing the old Committee. And when he got to my name there was a mumbling from one or two people and a distinct booing from the end of the back row. As Whittaker said something about 'our sincere thanks' a man jumped up and shouted: "Thanks, be damned!" It was the one who'd been booing, I felt sure, a burly loud-mouthed moron who lived in Horton Close, not all that far away from me. Masterson was his name.

"I say, that's a bit... I mean, the Committee have...." began Whittaker, floundering.

"I'm not saying nothing about the Committee," cut in Masterson, "I daresay they've done a good job. Except for one of 'em – and you all know who I'm referring to!"

"This is rather, er, ... Are you proposing a motion, Mr... er?" bumbled Whittaker.

"No, I'm not. Least, I wasn't, But since you're asking, I reckon there's a motion that ought to have been put long before now."

"Oh?"

"Yeah, and that's the motion that we get rid of a certain person – one who isn't sitting a hundred miles away from you, Mr. Whittaker!"

More rumbling, and a not-so-subdued 'hear hear'.

"I don't know what...."

"I bet you do, Mr. Headmaster. Don't tell me you don't know nothing about what your Mr. Whitehouse gets up to!"

"Really, I. This is not the proper place. I must ask you to sit down, Mr. er, and let the Chairman, er ...."

"I reckon there's been too much sitting back and letting things go from bad to worse. It's time somebody spoke up. It's time the guilty party was challenged to stand up and take what's coming to him!"

There were several more 'hear-hears' at this and a noise that almost amounted to a roar of approval.

"That's right! What about our children? In the hands of a lunatic like *him!*" Screeched a woman. Shouts of agreement.

Whittaker looked dazed. The meeting was completely out of hand.

Suddenly, I noticed Wheate get up and make for the exit. But, no.

He'd stopped, level with Masterson, and was staring at him. Masterson turned to him and appeared to recoil a little, rather like a bull in mid-charge that suddenly feels the prick of a dart. Then Wheate, for some unguessable reason, looked down at his own feet, shook his head as though he'd just changed his mind about something, and hurried out of the hall. Later, I was to learn the explanation of all this.

Masterson went back to his work of rabble-rousing with renewed vigour. Whittaker argued feebly with him, though I doubt whether either of them could hear a word the other was saying on account of the din from the people in between. Odd, that I should be noting all these things like an uninvolved spectator – it was me they were all attacking! Everybody had some nasty remark to make, each person was determined to trump his neighbour's accusations concerning me.

"Chuck him out, I say!" yelled Masterson, above the rest. We don't want his kind in our school!"

"Or in our village!" screamed a well-dressed hag.

Masterson lumbered down to the front, up to the Committee table, waving his beefy arms.

"Get out, you dirty pervert! Get out!" he shouted into my face. I pushed my chair back and scrambled to my feet. Masterson was about to hit me, I could see that. Some instinct told me, absurdly, to get up – get up so that I could be knocked down!

"Masterson! Masterson!" It was Wheate, back again, holding Masterson's shoulder. "Telephone, Mr. Masterson!"

"Sod the 'phone! I'm busy!"

"Your wife, Mr. Masterson. Urgent," said Wheate, in a matter-of-life-and-death voice.

A change came over Masterson's heavy purple features. "Oh? The wife, is it? Oh, ar. All right then. All right, I'm coming." And with a sigh he abandoned his role as mob orator, and left the hall at a brisk waddle.

The noise died down at his departure, and to my relief everybody subsided into their seats. The menacing note faded into mere grumbling, the traditional rhubarb-rhubarbing of disorderly meetings.

167

Finding my forehead clammy with sweat, I wiped it on my pocket handkerchief.

The election of the new Committee was an anti-climax. Needless to say, I was not nominated. Any Other Business fizzled out in no time. The meeting was declared closed, and the hall emptied in less than a minute.

Only Whittaker and the newly-elected Chairman, a fellow called Hurst, were still chatting amid the scattered papers as I left. Neither of them wished me goodnight. They simply looked through me.

I let the hall doors swing to behind me and set off along the corridor. But I didn't get far. Edmund Wheate was blocking the way.

Chapter 29

WHEATE opened the door to one of the classrooms and beckoned me.

"In here," he said. I pulled my glasses down to the end of my nose and stared at him as much as to say 'Who are you ordering about, my good man?' He stood quite still, holding the door wide, expectantly. I shrugged and walked in. After groping around for the light switch, I found it. Wheate was already sitting at the teacher's desk. Surely he hadn't meant us to talk in the dark?

"Sit down," he invited. Blasted nerve! Treating me as if I were a parent coming to see him on Open Evening, and he were the master!

It was on the tip of my tongue to ask him what all this was in aid of. I'd had just about enough for one evening, without being quizzed by a school Manager! Actually I said nothing. I just sat waiting for Wheate to talk.

"You're not a very happy man, George," he said at last. This really annoyed me. I wanted to wipe the solemn, solicitious look off his damned face! Of all the bloody effrontery! Who did he think he was? Then I recalled something Whittaker had been saying in the Staff room, about Wheate being a psychologist. Yes, that was it, a psychologist attached to one of the big Midland hospitals.

"Ah, shades of your profession, I suppose," I sneered. "The old headshrinker's couch, and all that."

He wagged his head from side to side at this, just as I do myself when faced with some piece of invincible ignorance in class. My temper rose. But before I could say anything, Wheate thrust his head forward and growled at me:

"You haven't a clue, have you? You're not happy, as I said, You're

169

completely unaware of your position, of the danger you're in. And you don't even realise what might have happened to you a few moments ago!"

"Oh, well it was just lucky that Masterson's wife called him."

"She didn't. I made it up. And fortunately for you he imagined she'd hung up, and went straight *home.*"

"Ah, well that's different. Thank you," I said, simply and nobly. "Very kind of you. But why?"

"Because I decided that was the best way to handle him."

This wasn't what I meant, but I let it go. I'd no wish to prolong this time-wasting business any further. I glanced ostentatiously at my watch.

"All right," I said. "I've expressed my gratitude, Mr. Wheate. But now, unless you've anything else to...."

"Else? I haven't started yet!" said Wheate. This is going to take more than a couple of minutes. I'm going to straighten you out!"

"Very well," I said. "I'll enrol as one of your patients, provided of course that there's no fee. But at this very moment I'm going home. Goodnight!"

I sprang to my feet and marched out. At least that was what I imagined I was going to do. But something had gone wrong. I glared at Wheate. He was hunched over the desk, looking at me from under his eyebrows. I still hadn't moved from my chair. With a shock, I discovered *I couldn't!*

Wheate continued to look at me, and there was a glint in his jet-black eyes that I didn't like at all. He didn't speak. I wanted to shout at him, curse and swear at him. But I didn't.

At once, the anger died in me. It was replaced by a new feeling, one utterly strange. I recognised it as the feeling of *awe.*

I suddenly saw the tremendous gulf that lay between myself and Wheate, between my posturings in 'consecrated circles' and what he had just done. My self-confidence went out of me like air out of a pricked balloon. I was only a sham. *He* had the real power.

Wheate spread his hands on the table and exhaled slowly. "Good.

170

We can begin," he said. "Now, listen carefully, George. Relax your body, open your mind. There'll be none of the old 'keep your eye on my gold watch' business. I simply want you to follow me closely. Are you ready?"

In my mind I replied 'Go to blazes!" but with my lips – and this was a most peculiar thing – I said, "Yes, I am." This dual, and quite contradictory, response was to persist through a large part of our talk.

"I said I would straighten you out," went on Wheate, "and I intend to do this. I'm not referring to your surface problems, your being a target of scandal, or your being on the brink of losing your job. I mean at your deepest level."

"Ah, the jolly old *id,*" I thought, recalling with scorn the psychological claptrap they'd fed us at Teacher Training college.

"I am not a Freudian," said Wheate, as if he'd read my mind, "but I do take a great interest in the workings of the subconscious. And in your case, George, it has been getting out of control. You have been attempting to bring the desires and dreams of your lower nature into the real world. You have lost sight of the borderline between fantasy and fact. Like a small child you are seeing life half as a story and half as it really is. You are hopelessly confused, George."

Inwardly I protested, outwardly I nodded meekly.

Wheate continued. He outlined, with an infuriating degree of accuracy, all my chief doings as a 'witch'. He explained my motives. Even in my mind I couldn't be bothered to argue any more. I just hadn't the strength. Perhaps he was right about me? The more he said, the more right he sounded. His voice ran steadily on, his Cork brogue agreeable to listen to, the tone of it thick and creamy, yet biting, like Guinness. I noted, incongruously, his marked resemblance to the Irish entertainer, Dave Allen. He had the same compulsive way of talking, the natural authority, the knack of phrasing that made you hang on his every word. He must have had what they call 'personal magnetism'.

As he went on and on listing my follies, I felt, while I listened, somehow coccooned, insulated from my surroundings, from everyday things, by a thick soft layer of cotton-wool.

171

"You've had completely the wrong idea of The Craft, George," he was saying. "It's nothing like that at all, nothing like it. Your 'dabbling-for-kicks' attitude is the very opposite of the true devotion."

This confused me a great deal. I was like a child trying to solve a problem quite beyond its years. The cotton-wool in my brain wouldn't allow me to grapple with it. It was like some distorted equation in which I had to balance Edmund Wheate, school Manager, on the one hand with The Craft, with a man who used the correct witches' term, with talk about the 'true devotion', on the other. With leaden clumsiness I tried fitting an 'equals' sign between the two, though I couldn't believe it. Or could I?

"Yes, The Craft, George. The recognition of the oldest primeval forces – the forces that Organized Religion ignores, or suppresses - the old gods. Yes, they exist, all right. As do their servants, their true servants, not meddling fools who know nothing! Yes, George, contrary to all appearances, *I am a witch.*"

I sat there horrified, as if the ground had opened up in front of my feet. Though this was ironical, for I was reacting in just the same way that innumerable village worthies had reacted when they'd heard the gossip about me!

"But I am not as you imagine," added Wheate. "I'm not a dabbler, but a genuine practioner. Nor do I meddle with evil power. I am a student of the *White* arts, never of the black!

"And because of my studies and my special knowledge, I am only too well aware of the danger that you, George, may have fallen into."

I was not impressed by this. Surely I was already in as much trouble as I possibly could be, with threats, bricks through my windows and so on?

"Danger, George. Not of the everyday, temporal, kind. Much worse. Spiritual danger! Yet you may have had a lucky escape.

"Boredom and lack of purpose led you to play at being a witch and this has led to your downfall. Though strangely enough this disgrace you're in may prove a blessing. It may have saved you from the real danger.

"Imagine, George, a small child playing with a sharp knife. To the child it is amusing, shiny and new, a toy. Until the razor-edge turns nasty and gashes him.

"The occult world is like that knife. There is the same appeal of the novel and strange. But there is a nastier edge! You, George, knew nothing of what you were doing, nothing of the forces lying just below the surface of ordinary life. You were perhaps even foolish enough to scoff at the idea of their very existence. But – and this is the terrifying thing – you could accidentally have made contact with them!

"Now, think back, George. What was your first step? I don't mean your overtures to potential members of your 'coven', I mean the first step inside your own mind."

I tried to think, if you could call it thought. My brain was so disorientated and sluggish that a single question seemed as demanding as a three-hour examination. Eventually, I came up with an image of a television screen, of nude dancers around a bonfire.

"There was a programme on the television," I said woodenly.

"Ah, the programme. A travesty! *I* provided material for that documentary, and they botched it! I, with all my contacts in covens up and down the country, prepared a demonstration of ritual. But the fools decided to use actors at the last minute! Those they interviewed were fakes. The whole thing was nothing but cheap sensational idiocy!

"So, you picked up all the wrong ideas from the start. A pity! There are many like you, George. And what happens to them? They sink lower and lower into malpractice until they reach their inevitable end: utter mental and physical breakdown.

"I am bound to give you the most solemn warning. You must never so much as incline your thoughts, even, towards occult matters again! Only those of perfect stability and wholeness of mind and will can venture safely into the realms of spirit. You, George, are not such a person. The adage of the ancients, 'know thyself', is as true today as ever. You ignored it. Not knowing yourself, not knowing what you wanted, you nearly strayed into the darkness. It is not for you. It is a life commitment. Leave it alone, George. Never tamper with it again.

"Do you understand me?"

I nodded dully.

"Then go," said Wheate quietly. "Go, and remember all that I've said to you, all except one thing, and that is a thing you have forgotten already."

I got up, walked out of the room like a robot, walked out of the school, across to the car park and unlocked my car. I leaned my head on the steering wheel, feeling completely drained.

Whittaker and Hurst appeared, got into their cars and drove off. A little later, Wheate did the same.

A long while after they'd gone, I raised sufficient energy to take myself home.

Chapter 30

ALTHOUGH I'd resigned, I expected I would have to work out the Autumn term at my school. Oh yes, I resigned. Not long after my talk with Edmund Wheate, in fact. Though it was not he who'd suggested it. He was not concerned with such mundane matters.

But for some reason the customary two months' notice was waived. I suspected some string-pulling on the part of the Managers, one of whom played golf with the Deputy Director of Education. No doubt all parties concurred on the advisability of getting rid of me as soon as possible.

So here I am, on the first day of September, on a train bound for London.

Hilary had merely shrugged at my decision. Her only stipulations were that I should continue to make her the same allowance, and that I should leave my standing orders at the bank for mortgage and so on, unaltered. I didn't even say goodbye to her. I couldn't, for when I left home to catch an evening train she was out.

I pressed my temple against the cold glass of the carriage window. A cluster of approaching lights must be Banbury, I guessed.

My briefcase lay across my knees and on top of it was the letter I'd received from *Falconhurst Hall, Private Day School in Exclusive Surroundings,* whose advert. I'd seen in the *Times Educational Supplement.*

I'd decided to spend the night in a hotel not far from Paddington Station, leaving myself only a Tube journey in the morning to the Middlesex suburb where the school was situated, rather than get up at the crack of dawn and arrive at the interview hotfoot from the Midlands. By the sound of their letter I was, to all intents and purposes, appointed already. The interview, I imagined, was a formality which they felt they ought to observe just in case I turned out to be either moribund, or a monster.equipped with fangs like Dracula. Reading between the lines I'd say that they were desperate. For despite their fancy names and flashy brochures, many of these private schools are cheapjack shoddy affairs. They charge high fees to gullible parents. They expect all books and stationery to be purchased on top of the fees. They employ all kinds of shady characters, "teachers" whose work would be called in question even in the most lackadaisical of State schools. But of course *I* couldn't afford to be choosy. And I felt pretty certain of this job, anyway. All I had to do was to make the right noises at the interview tomorrow, and I'd be teaching their little darlings in less than a week.

And so I was.

They were not such a bad lot on the whole. A little spoiled and petulant, and you couldn't give them any stick, even metaphorically, lest their doting parents took them away from the school. Members of staff were more or less told always to keep one eye on the customer.

My social life was dull in the extreme. I went to a Teachers' Club once a week, though God knows why. They were all much younger than me, except for one or two characters as ancient and fusty as Mr. Chips. I went to the cinema twice or even three times a week, always alone. I made no friends. It crossed my mind that I might perhaps pick up a woman. But the prospect of either descending into squalor with a grotty one, or suffering the wining, dining and husband-deceiving of an affair with a better-quality one, was enough to put me off the idea.

Out of sheer boredom I put more into my teaching than I'd done for many years, marking and preparing out of school hours, with the result that my pupils showed exceptional progress. I actually became the Headmistress's blue-eyed boy, and also received a number of unsolicited tributes from parents when they arrived to collect their offspring at the end of the day.

But as for weekends and evenings, I merely existed. I was about as lively as a zombie.

176

I'd been at *Falconhurst* about a month, I should think, when I heard from Hilary. Her letter was in a parcel of things I'd asked her to send on. It was three pages long, where it would not have surprised me if I'd had no letter at all, or at the most a few lines asking for a bigger allowance.

After explaining why she'd not enclosed all the things I wanted, she went on to give me what appeared at first to be a purely gratuitous report on the latest doings in the village.

'You might as well be dead,' she wrote, 'as far as people in this road are concerned. You're simply never mentioned. All the talk at the moment is about Ken Boulton – you know who I mean – his wife Joy used to come round to Shirley's next door quite a lot until they fell out. Well, he's run off with another woman. Only a young girl, no more than 20. And he must be over 40, and leaving Joy and the four kids. You can imagine how they're all going on about him!'

Yes, I could imagine it, with no effort at all.

'You'll probably be surprised, George, to hear that I hardly ever go out any more, especially as you remember I used to gad about a bit. Molly Batters seems to have taken a dislike to me, so I don't see anything of the Batters these days. Freddie still wants to be my friend, but one can't really put back the clock, can one? As for the girls I used to have coffee with, well, I was hurt at first when they stopped inviting me round, but now I realise their friendship was never really worth all that much.'

You're damned right, it wasn't! The only reason they ever cultivated you was so that they could pump you about me, or give you the latest gossip about me, or gush over you in false sympathy! Now that I am no longer in the spotlight they don't want you. You're redundant!

There were a few more lines in this same vein. They all added up to one thing: Hilary was lonely and feeling sorry for herself. She was as badly off, after all, as I was myself.

The weeks dragged on. And then, not long before Christmas, I had another letter from Hilary, in which she mentioned she'd be coming up

177

to London the following Saturday. She made it sound as though the whole object of her visit was to buy clothes, with just a mention at the end that we might possibly meet.

Beneath the take-it-or-leave-it note on which she concluded I wondered if perhaps she really did want to meet me. Might have been imagination on my part. Anyhow, I gave her a time and place and said I'd wait for her.

Walking through the streets of London's West End I had for a fleeting instant a total recall of a similar December evening many years before, eighteen or nineteen, I should think. I felt the same sense of expectancy, responded in precisely the same way to the bright lights, the smart folk hurrying about, the restaurant smells and the exotic aroma of cigars. Undiluted corn, of course! Probably no more than a view through the eyes of novelists I'd read in my impressionable teens.

I'll not try to romanticize the tramps in Leicester Square. Long ago, the newspapers they sat reading would have been kept to wrap themselves in against the night's chill. Now, if they slept out they'd be arrrested.

I sat on a bench next to one. But I moved when he started whining for the inevitable 'price of a cuppa.' The self-pity in his voice sickened me. It reminded me too much of myself.

I wandered about, hands in pockets, glancing at people as they appeared from the direction of the Tube. I was beginning to wonder if Hilary would turn up, after all. Then I saw her, walking towards me.